THE SHEPHERD INTO HELL

JOSEPH NORRIS III

DEDICATION

My mother, my wife, my son and my daughter, this book is dedicated to you. For enduring years of my spewing forth frighteningly bizarre ideas for stories, I am sincerely grateful. To my "cuz", the late Lowry Brooks, Jr, you truly shared my vision for the horrific, the terrifying, and the possibility of the stories created in my "brain factory", thank you. Dr. Eugenia Collier, Morgan State University, thank you for the formal training, and support, during my time spent in your wonderful creative writing class, and beyond.

CONTENTS

ACKNOWLEDGMENTS

To the following people, for whom I owe a debt of gratitude, for listening to and reading my "creepy" stories, and encouraging me, all along the way: Baltimore City College High School family, Cheyney University of Pennsylvania family, the Norris family, the Middleton family, Katrina Brown, and a gracious online family/fan following thank you.

The collaborative efforts of Editor, and Literary Consultant, Cryss A. Jones, Collective Press®, Danae Prosthetics® Photography, and Graphic Cover Design, and Chrita Paulin, Coal Under Pressure Publications™, without whom this book would probably still be a thought, thank you.

1 ROUTINE

Blood drippings are easy to follow through the woods. Randy's ass ran, so I shot him. Being a Bounty Hunter is fun, but a pain in the ass at times. Like now. You know, like chasing this knucklehead Randy through the damned woods, as it's getting dark. I want to get this job done, collect my money, and get home in time to watch the football game tonight.

I start to call Shaun, my partner, on the two-way radio when I hear Randy trudging through the woods. Shaun's at home and he knows I'm tracking Randy alone. All I need to do is update him, but it can wait.

"Randy! I know I hit you in your leg. You can't go far!"

In the distance to my left, away from where I heard Randy, I hear something else. Something heavy, stepping on the brush. Maybe Randy has an accomplice, or maybe it's a damned bear.

"I can't believe I'm doing this shit. Good thing the money for this one is right for me." I say to myself, as I start off in the direction I heard Randy, but I'm keeping a wary lookout in the direction of that other sound.

I see less blood on the ground now and these drippings look strange to me. It's as though Randy smeared them or tried to wipe them away. Perhaps he just covered his wound, but the droplets just don't look right.

"Randy!" I yell.

"Fuck you, you cripple!" He yells back.

I smirk at his response, a jab at my disability: the amputation of my right leg from a gone wrong military extraction, at an unnamed location. That never stopped me from getting my man or woman.

Couldn't hide this shit; hell, the whole world saw this version of my story. Joe Cocamoe, Army Ranger, blown the fuck up saving squad, but he survived. National-ass news. A bounty hunter gig is the only thing that helps me pay my bills, after losing my leg. I had to prove myself daily, when I started hunting, just to show everyone I could handle myself. That was

1

until Terre Haute, Indiana, when I beat the crap out of one of my bounties with my prosthetic leg, while hopping around on my real one. That scared the snot out of everyone who witnessed it, but it gave me much street cred.

"This cripple is turning your now-crippled ass in today!" I shout.

Right now, though, I'm having a problem. My body weight is causing my prosthetic leg to get stuck in this calf-deep muck of mud, leaves, and twigs. This shit's slowing me down and making me tired. A fallen tree helps me pull myself free of this crap, so I can take a quick rest.

"Shit, Cocamoe, you didn't tell me you have a dog working with you!" Randy shouts.

My brow furrows. I gauge the distance and direction of his voice, which I estimated to be a100 or so yards due east.

"I don't do dogs. You gotta feed them things!" I shout, positioning my ass better on this beat down tree.

Maybe that's what I heard earlier: a dog, it smeared Randy's blood on the leaves with its paw or licked the leaves or some crazy shit like that.

"Damn homie, this is one ugly, big ass dog. What you feed this mother….!!!" Randy yells.

His yells quickly evolve into screams, coupled with loud grunts, growls, crunching, and shit being ripped. Swinging my legs quickly over the downed tree, I hit a firm spot on the ground and hurry towards the sounds, with my trusty Glock™ 9mm drawn. The closer I get to Randy, the more gruesome the sounds become. Loud thrashing, moaning, then quick whimpering gurgles, followed by brute crunching and chomping sounds. My approach is now very hesitant. There's an area where I can crouch behind a large tree for cover.

I'm about twenty to thirty feet away from Randy, and this thing. Not really sure what I'm looking at. Visibility is good even though it's dusk, and many intrusive clouds fight against the bright quarter moon. That, within itself, can make the woods' shadows play visual tricks on you. But, this ain't no damned shadow.

On top of Randy is this large wolf-like thing. Covered with thick dark gray and black fur. It's about seven to eight feet in length on all fours with its front paws astraddle Randy's stomach. Its head shakes deep inside of Randy's open shredded chest. Through squirting blood and pieces of Randy's insides flying around, I can make out some of this thing's facial features; both animal and human, wrinkled, worn, and withdrawn skin. Patches of longer black fur dangle from the creature's face and it's long pointed ears, reminding me of a Gargoyle atop old European buildings. Randy is making an effort to fight this monster off, raising his left arm to strike a blow to only have it quickly wrenched off his shoulder with one swift bite. It constantly takes bites out of Randy with those large sharp teeth, making Randy's body jump violently and quiver spastically, with each vicious chomp. Anger and rage live prominently in this thing's dark yellow, almond-shaped eyes. Each bite expels blood-red clouds of frost, as its hot breath mixes with the crisp autumn air. I'm scared and pissed. Scared because I don't know what the fuck this thing is and pissed because it's eating my damned money.

From my already crouched position, I shoot. The first couple of hits are straight body shots propelling this beast right off Randy. But it gets up quickly looking straight at me. Its back arches upward, it belches out a wicked grunt and rockets to me. I stand my ground and fire several shots to its head, four more to the body, but it doesn't stop or slow down.

This creature leaps hard on top of me, sending us crashing backward, falling to the cold, muddy ground. My fast reaction has my right arm shielding myself. Somehow, I manage to pull out my knife with my other hand, stabbing its chest, legs, head, everywhere, anywhere, repeatedly.

The weight of this wolf-like thing feels like it's breaking my arm and the right side of my upper body burns like a motherfucker. A hard pain in my chest almost causes me to faint, making movement and breathing unbearable, but I can't let this thing kill me. Feels like some of my ribs are broken. Our struggle feels like it lasts forever. This "animal" makes many furious attempts to devour me: shaking its head violently from left to right; snarling and snapping its teeth at my head, face, and neck; anything to get a hold of me. It's hot, slimy saliva, coupled with Randy's blood, splatters all over my head and face. Its foul breath has a smell of stale cabbage and rotted meat, almost choking me into submission. My death grip on the thick, coarse, furry throat of this beast is the only thing keeping me alive, so far.

One of its large front paws presses hard against my chest, jutting my damaged ribs further into my insides, to the point where I almost puke. At the same time, the creature's hind legs scrape and claw at my legs. Pawing my artificial leg hard, it rips and tears the synthetic cover. Claws hit my carbon fiber pylon. It hesitates, looks strangely at me for a second, then continues its quest to eat me. All the while, my stabbings never stop, nor does my adrenaline rush to survive.

Abruptly, much like it started, our struggle stops. The beast lies atop me, breathing rapidly, then methodically slow. Steam rises up from the wounds I've inflicted. It's still hard for me to breathe and move, but I get enough strength to push it off of me and sit up from my waist. On my ass, I'm moving awkwardly and fast as I can to get away. My head and shoulders bang into something hard sticking out of the ground. A little stunned, I reach behind me. I feel the hard, cold stiff contours of a big ass boulder. I lay my upper back against it, watching in disbelief at that wolf-like thing that's trying to get away from me. Scurrying away, like that live crab that jumps out of the boiling pot.

Its head dangles, really fucked up looking, hard to the left. Partially decapitated from my flurry of knife blows. I see its blood oozing freely from my hacking.

I try getting to my extra clip to load it, but I can't raise my arm, nor reach my two-way radio. Vapid pain in my right arm has me look down to see the deep bloody rip next to a bite.

"Shit, that fucking thing bit me!"

While trying my best to assess what's just happened, I take a quick look over to my right to see what's left of Randy. Some of him is still salvageable, at least. Hell, all I really need to collect my bounty is his face anyway. Further away from me, but still visible, a low groan comes from that wolf-like thing. Instinctively, I point my gun in that direction and fire. After several loud quick empty clicks, I stop. Damned gun's empty.

That's when I realize I need to get up off this ground and really gather myself. Pushing my head and upper shoulders against the boulder for leverage, I fight to pull myself off the ground. Millions of stinging, tightening sensations shooting through my right side add to my struggle. Wrenching in absolute pain, my mind fights hard with my body for it to straighten itself. My mind wins, but not without a few blows from my body. Shit. More blood drips down my right arm. Standing upright, I feel another sharp stinging sensation. This one, in my right stump, making me lurch hard to my left. Luckily, I'm able to lean heavily against the boulder with my good leg to keep from toppling over. My battle with that thing made my prosthetic leg twist sideways within my socket, causing the pain in my stump. I attempt to straighten it out but fail miserably; it doesn't fit properly so it has to come off so I can adjust it. What the hell else can go wrong?

More sounds from that wolf-like thing seize my attention. Another low groan and what again sound like bones breaking with some pounding onto the ground. Like an idiot, I limp toward the sounds, but not before finally managing to load the extra clip into my gun. Thankfully, my heavenly stage lighting is still with me and I see a gully, about 15 feet in front of me. That's where the sounds are coming from. My limp is now more of a hop and drag, with labored breathing, and knife-like stabbing pain with every movement. Finally, when making it to the edge of the gully, I look down not seeing a thing. Then I catch slight movement to my left.

"What the fuck!?"

Below me is what appears to be a naked man, or at least what's left of a man anyway! It has animal legs and partial face of that wolf-thing that attacked me. It's slowly transforming into a full human, with its head still dangling, resting silently sideways on its left shoulder. Its spinal cord protruding from its body spurts out blood.

Its sullen eyes are closed. When all of a sudden, they spring open, its chest expands hard for breath, scaring the hell out of me. Adrenaline dulls the pain in my right arm, and I shoot. My wavering from my prosthetic not fitting properly has me fall to the stupid ass ground, but not before I fire more bullets into its body.

Sitting up painfully fast, I knock my two-way radio out of my vest pocket onto the ground. Weakened, I slowly pick it up with my left hand to call Shaun.

"Shaun, come in Shaun, this is Cocamoe!" I yell, excitedly, still eyeing that wolf-like thing.

"Yeah, what up," Shaun responds, in a chilled relaxed tone.

"Man, I'm down…. I got Randy though, he's down too. I'm still in Seawell State Park. Track me with the GPS! Make it fast…. bring a body bag and some gloves!"

"Ok, got you. body bag and gloves. Be there soon. You gonna be ok?" Shaun said, his tone now shifting toward urgency.

"Yeah, I think so. Just hurry."

My gun has a few bullets left and my knife is ready. I begin wrapping my wound with part of my torn shirt, thinking how a big muscular motherfucker like me got taken down so easily by that wolf-like thing. My six- foot three, 235-pound frame fell like a damned brick. I'm also thinking of what to tell Shaun as to why Randy is half-eaten, why I'm beaten down like this, and what's the deal with the naked dead man in the gully. I've got maybe forty-five minutes to an hour before Shaun gets to me from his house, so this story had better be good. I just know the truth was a no go.

With time to waste, I fumble with my pants to get them undone. I ease down the right side of my pants to get done what needs to be done, adjust my prosthetic with one hand. This ain't going to be easy, as my prosthetic is held tight onto my upper leg with a thick silicone sock and neoprene sheath. These devices provide major suction to keep them connected to my body and they work amazingly. Even though my stump is moving around way too much in my socket, the prosthetic stayed on during my fight and fall with that wolf-like thing.

Anguishing from the pain in my right arm, I unhook my prosthetic sheath to pull it off my stump. The silicone sock is harder to get off because it's wet and yucky from my sweat, making it stick tighter to the skin of my upper thigh. Determination and the need for relief enable me to get the sock and socket off with just using my left hand. Instantly, I place both items between my legs and start massaging my entire stump feeling for abrasions or cuts. Gladly none are found. All feels fine except my knee. It feels a little funky. That goes away after I finagle the silicone sock back on by rolling it up my stump, moving it up onto my thigh. The socket is easy to get on, just need to make physical adjustments.

Standing up straight, my body weight sinks my stump further into the socket. Moving around slightly then standing still makes it all feel much better. To get the neoprene sleeve rolled fully on, I roll it up my prosthetic and onto my upper thigh, slowly and gingerly. Now to see if this shit works and if that wolf-thing is still there.

Sighing heavily, I take one step forward, then another, followed by two more. A slight limp but walking is doable. In a few minutes, I'm back at the edge of the gully looking at the man-wolf-demon, or whatever it is. I go back to the boulder to sit, waiting for Shaun. Checking my two-way I see it's near midnight. Might as well relax or try to. Hoping no more fuckers like that thing in the gully are out here.

A beam from a large spotlight in the distance moves fast toward me. Nervousness sets in, 'cause that might not be Shaun. Waiting until the beam gets about 100 yards away from me, I aim my gun towards it.

"State your business!" I yell.

No answer.

"State your business! State your business now or I'm shooting!" I yell.

"Dude it's me, Shaun, calm your ass down!" Shaun yells back.

Lowering the gun, my left arm is tired and limp. If I had fired, I probably would've missed anyway.

"You look worse than shit dude," Shaun said, coming upon my haggard, disheveled self.

My makeshift wrapping, the blood/mud/saliva mix covering my face, and other parts of my body have him break out the first aid kit fast. As I undo my makeshift wrapping with my left hand, Shaun looks again at my right arm, shining the spotlight on it.

"Shit man, is that a bite? Who, or what bit you?"

I point to the area where the gully and the naked wolf-thing are. Shaun looks at me, gets up and walks over to the gully. He shines his spotlight down and around the gully, then walks back to me.

"Ain't shit down there."

Looking up at Shaun, my first instinct is to drag him back over there, but I can't. Too weak. I exhale, head motioning to Shaun to place Randy in a body bag as I point in another direction in this forest of death. He points his spotlight in that direction.

"What the hell! Dude, you went cannibal on him!" Shaun exclaimed, looking at the grossed-out mold of Randy.

"His ass was like that when I found him; guess a bear, mountain lion or wolf had dinner!"

Shaun smushes his face and puts on the rubber gloves to place Randy's pieces in the body bag.

"If you found him like this, then how'd you get all effed up?" Shaun asked.

"He had someone with him, I shot him. He fell in the gully. Guess whatever got Randy got his ass too. I just happened to be very lucky

6

tonight." I said, placing antiseptic on my wound, still trying to gather myself mentally.

"Yeah, ok. Your type of luck sucks. Dude, we better get you to a hospital to check out that wound, bite, whatever it is. You might have rabies or HIV."

I nod agreeing to go to a hospital, but only if we go collect my money when done there.

"Can you walk to the truck?" Shaun asked.

"Yeah, I've got it," I said.

"Damn, man! Randy feels real nasty in the bag, real damned nasty!" Shaun said, slinging the body bag over his right shoulder.

"Carry the bag or me, dammit!"

Shaun mumbles something under his breath, steadying the body bag. He points his spotlight ahead of us with me taking the lead. I'm worn and beat down but not stupid. I'd rather see any further attacks head-on than from behind.

As we walk, I notice how eerily quiet the woods are. I know the animals are aware of our presence, it was still too damned quiet. They know something we don't.

Shaun stops walking, exhaling heavy behind me.

"How you making out, dude?" he asked.

"I'm fine, be better when I get my money. You seem like you need this break. I'd rather not stop so let's go."

"Hold up dude. I just thought about this. Where's your truck?"

"Other side of the park, we can pick it up tomorrow.... oh, make that later that today," I said, checking the time on my two-way.

Shaun nods and we continue walking. Within a few minutes, we're right next to his truck. Randy's body, thrown by Shaun, makes several dull sounding thuds as it careens off the floor of the truck's back bed compartment. I gaze at Shaun.

"What?" asked Shaun.

"Never mind," I said, shaking my head, looking around the area because of the racket Shaun made. I'm still a tad fidgety over the shit that happened with Randy.

The nearest hospital, Northeastern, is only five miles away. I figure we could get there quickly, get myself checked out, then go get my money for this hard-fought, strange ass bounty. Randy's truck door is truly heavy so opening it slowly was no problem for me. Quickly hoping in, a problem. My quick sudden movement sends spikes of pain through my abdomen, chest, and arm. Shaun quickly comes to my aid, gently placing my legs fully into the cab of the truck.

"You ok?"

My grimace is my answer. With my eyes shut, I hear the truck driver's side door open. Shaun flops into the seat and starts the engine. My eyes are still closed until I realize I don't have my seat belt on. Shaun watches me struggle with the connection, so he reaches over and clicks it for me. My eyes close again when I feel the truck move along. Images of that wolf-like thing eating Randy crawl into my head, getting quicker by the second. Its attack of me, its size, teeth, blood, and rancid smell. That naked near decapitated dying human thing.

Flashing open, my eyes are unfocused, unable to determine my surroundings. Up ahead, I see a blurry large bright red neon EMERGENCY sign erasing the darkness. Looking over at Shaun, my vision gets a little better and I see he's on his cell phone. No wonder there weren't a million questions coming from him, he's in "get booty mode". He notices me, so he gets off the phone. Parking the truck in the ER ambulance designated spot.

Once parked, he hops out and runs around in front of the truck to the passenger side to get to me. By the time he gets to my side, I've already eased open the door and was slowly sliding out of the chair. My movement is stiff yet the pain and discomfort I had earlier aren't as arresting. There's a look of disappointment on Shaun's face, as he wanted to show he can fully take care of me, his 'big brother'.

"I told you. I got this. You know you can't park here" I said, walking to the ER ambulance entrance foyer.

"Well, tonight I'm an ambulance and a hearse," Shaun said.

He reaches down inside the rear of the truck, patting the body bag.

"You stay right there, we'll be right back," Shaun said, pulling his hand back fast, and wiping it on his pants leg.

The ER ambulance entrance foyer has two sets of sliding doors. One set facing the parking lot, the other set facing the inside of ER itself, away from the waiting room. I'm already in the middle of the foyer when Shaun races in by my side.

"Damn, you're fast when you wanna be," he mumbles.

I bluntly stop at the inner door leading inside the ER. Shaun stops too. He looks around in all directions with his hand on his gun.

"Dude. What's wrong? Who you see?"

"No one. I forgot, she's probably working tonight. Take me to Morgan General instead." I said, standing there, as both sliding doors open and close without stopping.

"Dude. You're talking about April? So, what if she's here, she can take care of you." Shaun said.

"I don't want her freaking out and asking me a million and one questions."

"Hey! You two! You're letting the cold air in!" a voice screams out.

It was her. April, my girlfriend for the last five years. She's a Nurse

Practitioner, working the ER tonight. We've been off and on during our five-year run-this so happens to be one of our "off" times. I frown when turning to face her. When she sees me and my condition, the rapid-fire questions begin on cue.

"Shaun? Cocamoe? What the hell happened to you!? Why didn't you call me!? Shaun, what did y'all do!?"

All her commotion gets the attention of the ER staff and the few patients present.

"I'll take this priority; you guys take what you have and the few in the waiting room. I'm taking room 9!" April blurts out, commanding her team.

"Do you need help?" a female voice yells out.

"No, I'm good," April said.

Before I could get any words out, Shaun begins telling her everything. By this time, April has taken my left elbow gently, leading me and Shaun into empty exam room 9. He's yet to stop yapping.

April pushing me slightly onto a gurney calls on her hospital two-way radio for a Dr. Seti to come to ER exam room 9. She gives me a regimented visual exam, not saying a word to either of us.

"Some of this blood ain't mine," I said.

She raises her eyebrows, goes to the cabinet getting fresh gauze, antiseptic, tape, and scissors to dress and clean my wound and bruises. Shaun, still going off at the mouth, helps April remove my bloody shirt and vest. Now he's telling parts of the story that didn't even happen. Always exaggerating around women.

".... then there was this big ass explosion...." Shaun was saying when I slowly cut my eye at him.

"Okay, maybe not as big of an explosion as I thought."

April, half listening to Shaun's tale, was fully engaged with the details of her work - no time to play the role of concerned girlfriend....one of the reasons for the pendulous relationship.

"Cocamoe, why didn't you take Shaun with you if this guy was that dangerous?" April blurts out.

"Shit, that stings!" I said, reacting to alcohol applied to my arm's wound.

"Stop pulling away."

"You pull away, woman. Shit, Randy wasn't dangerous, it was his partner that snuck me!"

April pulls my arm closer to her to tend to my injury. Shaun was going to say something but shuts up when a doctor enters the room.

"Hi, Dr. Seti. Mr. Cocamoe is a Fugitive Recovery Specialist. He was out on a job and got attacked. He has lacerations on his right forearm, and what appears to be a bite. The patient also complains of right upper quadrant pain in the rib and sternum areas, and right abdominal tenderness, on palpation, I'm going to call x-ray and transport."

Dr. Seti gets closer to examine me.

"Bounty hunter? Went bad huh? Tell me if this hurts when I touch this area."

Dr. Seti places a finger on my right upper abdomen. Grimacing, I pull away. He then lifts my right arm slowly; and then down, checking my range of motion. Now in more pain, I'm close to decking him.

"Mr. Cocamoe, is it?" Dr. Seti asked, releasing my arm.

I roll my eyes.

"What happened?" Dr. Seti asked.

Shaun, once again is about to speak, when I quickly said,

"Just like the lady said Doc. I went out on assignment. Chased a client through the woods. I found the client dead, his partner ambushed me. I fought him off, he bit me, and I shot him. Now I'm here."

Dr. Seti looks at my right arm again, looks at me, then turns to April.

"April, get CT Chest, Abdomen, and Pelvis, too. Then you can get Mr. Cocamoe prepped for rabies shots…"

"Rabies, why rabies shots. A man bit me not a dog!" I shout.

"Mr. Cocamoe, this bite looks like an animal bite, we'll first have some blood drawn to be sure, then maybe the rabies shots."

"I've had them before Doc, not pleasant."

"Good, then you would only have to get one shot. Just to be cautionary."

Dr. Seti takes a closer look at my chart.

"You're an amputee? Are you diabetic?"

By now I've gotten more irritated with all the jibber-jabber from this damned quack and April. I just want them to do what needs to be done so I can get the hell out of here and get my money.

"NO! Leg was blown the fuck off doing a military assignment doc!"

The room gets quiet. April and Shaun stare at me. She has that "you're an asshole" look on her face while Shaun tries to hide his grin. Dr. Seti smiles looks me straight in the face, and says,

"Yeah. I remember you now, war vet. Semper Fi!"

"I was an Army Ranger, Dr. Veterinarian."

Dr. Seti puts my chart down, turns away from me leaving the room hurriedly.

"That wasn't right, you jerk!" April yells.

"Yeah man, not cool." Shaun chimes.

"Whatever! Just fix me up so I can get out of here and get my money. "

Shaun sheepishly turns away from me, acting like he's reading the medical poster about diabetes on the wall. I wrench again in pain as April dresses my wound.

"Be careful, dammit," I said, clenching my teeth.

"Big ass baby."

Before I could make another remark, the "blood nurse", or Phlebotomist, comes into the room. I've always thought of them as vampires.

"Hi, Sara."

"Hey April"

"Sara this is Mr. Cocamoe. Dr. Seti wrote the order for blood work to be done on him please."

"No problem. How are we doing Mr. Cocamoe?" Sara asks while unfolding her vampire tools.

I say nothing. Shaun, on the other hand, was going to say something, again, but I stopped him... again.

"She's got a job to do and so do you. Go check on Randy."

"What? He ain't going no...."

"Go, Now!" I quickly said.

The ladies look at the two of us briefly, then continue doing what they are there to do. Shaun huffs leaving the room.

2 BAIL BONDSMAN

Time in the hospital took longer than expected. Blood was drawn, x-rays were done, one rabies shot, bite cleaned and dressed. No broken bones, just a lot of bruises and soreness, and a doggie bag of meds given to me by April. I'm now free to go do what I really want. My fight with April will probably continue when she gets off later today, so I'll have some time to prepare. This wrap they placed across my chest was almost too tight, having me walk more awkwardly than before to Shaun's truck. Once there, I slap him on the bill of his baseball cap to wake him.

"Man, what's your problem. You screwed up my dream of me and that blood nurse." Shaun said, agitated.

"Stop being horny. We've got to get to The Store and then go get my truck." I said, motioning for Shaun to scoot over to the driver's side.

The Store is what we in the business call the bondsman agency. Shaun starts the truck as I ease in, taking a second to look in the back at the crumpled body bag. My head is still quite confused and fuzzy as to whether what happened really did happen.

"Sara is fine, isn't she?" I said, trying to clear my head by starting small talk.

"Who?"

"Sara, the vampire nurse from the hospital."

"Oh yeah, she sure is."

"Sorry, I cock-blocked."

Shaun looks at me, surprised that I apologized.

"No problem, no problem." He said, still gazing at me strangely.

Riding up Sansa Street, towards The Store, the low beat of House music rumbles through the truck. Limp dark clouds are at attention against the coming sun's burnt sky which, at times, turns the color backdrop a blood red. There's a lone figure standing in front of the gloomy void of a

13

forgotten shoe store. I try my best to focus on this figure, but I can't see too clearly. Agitation begins to set in when suddenly my vision becomes clearer. It's a man, changing. Changing into that thing from the woods, half human half wolf. Bloodied, as meat sloughs out of its mouth.

"Oh shit. Shaun, he's right there! Right there!" I shout.

Shaun hits the brakes hard, lurching us forward, tightening the seat belt around our waist and shoulders. Strangely, that move didn't hurt my chest as much as it should've. Shaun looks in the direction I'm looking in, then in the opposite direction.

"Who? I don't see anyone!" Shaun shouts.

Within seconds the man/wolf-thing is gone, the street is totally empty. I look again in each direction; the whole block is empty of people. Disoriented and confused I turn to Shaun.

"Nothing man, forget it. These meds are fucking with me." I said, lowering my head.

Of course, I was lying, I hadn't taken any meds, except that rabies shot. Shaun looks at me, then again out onto an empty Sansa Street. He looks at me again, then places the truck in drive. He wants to say something but he keeps it to himself.

We're four blocks from The Store. Actually name, 'Regency Bond Agency'. Those few blocks I keep my head low, not wanting to see that man/wolf-thing again, or Shaun's worrisome glances. I feel the truck slowing down.

"Cool, he's just opening," Shaun said.

The dashboard clock read 6:45 a.m. I see Derek, the Bondsman, bent over, pulling up the metal gate in front of his agency. I can smell his signature scent from the truck; cheap ass cigar. Weird, considering the windows are up and we're still about 100 or so feet away from him. I watch, as Derek's short stubby ass jumps up to push the remaining gate all the way up. His fake cheap Hawaiian shirt is not weather-appropriate and is too short. His belly roll is exposed when he jumps and when he stands still. His pudgy face tired, puffy, and always angry from fights with our government and his ex-wife. Hard to believe this fat little dude was a real badass during the Vietnam War. I don't tease or criticize him much; after all, he was the one that got me started with bounty hunting.

"Pull your shirt down or buy clothes that actually fit," I yell, rolling down the truck window.

"Kiss my Green Beret ass."

Shaun has parked and already gotten out of the truck, holding the body bag in his hands like dry cleaning, fussing and cussing under his breath. I slowly get out and limp up to Derek.

"Damn, Cocamoe, who kicked your ass? No, don't tell me. April."

"Fuck you. Look, I've got someone for you and I want my money.

Shaun, come here."

Shaun steps forward, reaching down to unzip the body bag.

"Asshole. What the fuck? Not here. Inside. I ain't had my breakfast", Derek said, in his low gravelly tone, pushing Shaun's hand away from the body bag zipper.

Derek and I have a quick stare down, when he steps in front of me, pushing open The Store's front door for us to enter. Once inside, Derek flicks on the lights. Three large desks piled with documents, newspapers, fugitive clippings, cigar butts, food wrappers and a few condom packs greet us. Derek grabs the condom packs, placing them in his pocket.

"What about all that other shit?" I asked.

Derek ignores me.

"Here, put that over here," Derek said, taking a short stubby arm and with one swipe, clears one desk from its weeks' worth of trash.

Shaun throws Randy onto the desk with a muffled dull thud.

"What?' Shaun asked, referring to my sneer at him.

I say nothing, walking closer to where Randy is laid.

"So, who we got here?" Derek asked.

I unzip the bag with my left hand. Derek looks inside the near-empty bag, then to us.

"What? You did all this shit for an empty ass bag?"

Reaching in the bag, I pull out the slightly bloody arm that's semi-connected to a shoulder and three-quarters of a head. Derek looks at what's pulled out, walks around to get a full view, then walks calmly to one of the other desks. He opens the middle drawer, pulling out a small black box. Opening it, he pulls out a cigar, casually placing it in his mouth, lighting it.

"So. Who the fuck is that?' Derek asked while puffing.

I glance at the corpse, then at Derek.

"Its Randy, Randy Hood. You sent me to retrieve him. He jumped bail, his bounty $20,000."

"He's dead assholes, plus how in the hell do I know that's him?" Derek said, between puffs.

"It's him," I said.

Shaun snatches the fugitive poster out of his front shirt pocket, unraveling it. I'm still holding Randy, noticing my body movements have gotten better since coming into The Store. Not sure why, but I'm dealing with money now, so I'll worry about my body later. I position Randy's head, waving Derek's cigar puffs away. Then had Shaun shine his spotlight on the head, while I hold the fugitive poster next to Randy's horror encased face. Neither of us got squeamish about the sight of Randy. Derek and I saw far worse during our military tours and Shaun got used to seeing shit like this real quick.

"Dead ringer," I said, smiling.

Derek looks at both items, gets closer to get a better look, takes another puff of his cigar.

"Okay, fine. It's him. But why you fuck him up like that, Cocamoe?"

"Found him like that in the woods. His bond is twenty g's and I get 30% of that, so let's go."

"Whoa, whoa, whoa, hell no. Where'd you get 30% from?!"

"Yeah, I know you said 10% but since I almost got killed, the ante increased!"

"Almost died? Like I give a shit! That's part of your job. I ain't giving 30% of 20g's, hell no!!"

"Fine. Shaun, zip Randy up. I'll take him back where I got him from, and you can go into the woods and get him. Maybe what did this to him is still out there, hungry for fat little bondsmen."

Derek looks again at what's left of Randy before Shaun zips up the body bag.

"Wait. Wait a minute! Look Cocamoe, I know I said dead or alive, but he's really fucked up dead. How can I show him to my client like that?"

"Same damned way I showed you. Do I get my money or what?"

Derek curses, walks back to the desk he got the cigar from and pulls out a larger dark red box. He opens it and I see a shitload of cash along with a .45 automatic pistol. He raises the pistol towards us smiling then lays it down gently. Derek takes a wad of money out of the box and cautiously counts out some bills. When done, he walks up to us, extending his hand with the bills to me. Shaun reaches for the money then stops, backing away from Derek.

"Here, six thousand, now GET OUT!!"

I grab the cash then hand it to Shaun.

"Count it." I said.

Derek's about to blow up again. I place my finger over his plump lips as Shaun's counts out the one-hundred-dollar bills. When finished, he signals to me the correct amount is there. I half-ass salute Derek as we leave The Store.

"Shaun, run me to get my truck," I said, easing myself into the truck even though there is little pain. Just being cautious.

"Yes sir, anything you say, sir."

I know he gave that smart-ass compliant answer because he wants some of the money. Hell, he didn't do shit, but I gave him a thousand anyway. Of course, he's very happy with that.

"I'd say don't spend it all in one place but...."

"No sir-ee Bob, I got special plans for this cash."

Smiling, I sit further back in the seat to get some shuteye. That's undone by my cell buzzing in my pants pocket. I'm able to maneuver my body, in spite of this tight ass body wrap, to get it out. It's April. I don't answer, placing the cell in the pocket of the scrub shirt borrowed from the hospital.

Five minutes later it buzzes again.

"May as well answer it, dude."

I pull out the cell to turn it off.

Looking out of the truck window I see the entrance to Seawell State Park.

"Damn Shaun, how fast were you going?"

"Fast enough dude. Fast enough."

We pull up to my truck and stop.

"Cocamoe, can you drive?"

I look at him straight-faced.

"Fine time to ask!"

"Look, man, I can run you home and we can get the truck later 'cause you still look like shit."

I undo the seat belt and open the passenger door, easing myself out of his truck. The limp is still there, yet less pain. Getting to my truck, I open the door, wiggle my ass into the driver's seat start the engine and pull off. I say nothing to Shaun. My rear-view mirror shows him giving me the finger as his other hand holds the hospital bag with my bloody shirt and vest. A quick chuckle from me is overtaken by me instantly becoming more conscious of my surroundings, feeling uneasy.

Wanting to get out of the woods as quick as possible, I step on the accelerator speeding down Dunkirk Avenue. Without warning the man/wolf-thing pops up in front of my truck. I swerve to the left to avoid hitting it when I hear a car horn blaring from a car headed straight for me. Hitting the brakes, I turn my truck sharply to the right, awaiting the stinging jolt and loud sound of metal on metal colliding. Seconds pass, only screeching tires are heard along with the smell of burning rubber against asphalt, but no impact. My head turned and face lowered to avoid any flying glass. I hear a car door opening then slamming hard. A loud, angry, slightly recognizable voice follows.

"Your ass is mine!" it cries out, getting closer to the driver's side of my truck.

I'd better look up before I get shot or something. The voice belongs to Detective Norris. We've dealt with one another a few times at Northwest Police District. Could never forget his thrift store frumpy wardrobe. A wrinkled polyester tan sports jacket, white button-down shirt, wide vintage tie, unwashed black pants, complete with food and coffee stains. Bottomed out with worn brown walking shoes. He has yet to recognize me.

"Show me your license and registration now!"

My eyes roll as I reach under my visor to get my items. He takes them from me, looking at my driver's license, bounty hunter's license then my car registration.

"Oh, it's you, 'Mr. I don't need a warrant to kick your ass'."

"Yes, officer, err... Detective. I'm just coming from the hospital on my way home. The meds they gave me are starting to kick in, I'm very sorry sir."

Detective Norris looks inside my truck. Seeing the pharmacy bag; my arm bandaged, the hospital scrub shirt as well as the wrap around my chest, he pauses, gives me back my credentials leaning into my truck to get close to me.

"You know I don't like you too much. If it wasn't for the fact that my cousin Shaun works with you, and you being a Vet, I'd run your dumb ass in. Slow the fuck down and go home. Now!"

I'm not going to argue with him. I jab my licenses back under my visor and pull off slowly. Making sure not to sideswipe his car or hit him standing in the street.

A lot of crazy shit has happened to me in the last 24 hours.

3 HOME SWEET HELL

The clock in my truck reads 9:30 a.m. Not far from home now. Luckily, my neighborhood 's in a quiet, almost non-existent spot in Baltimore. Here, people don't bother each other and no one's too nosy. I love that my apartment complex is on the edge of beautiful Seawell State Park, the largest park in Baltimore, but now I'm kind of leery about its proximity to the city and the shit you can find in there.

Pulling into the parking lot, I feel much-needed serenity and peace. One of my downstairs neighbors, Carlito, is working on his car. Upbeat Latin tunes are wafting from his freshly polished chocolate brown Nova, with the (4.0 liter) Hemi engine. There are a few children out; boys and girls, on a warm autumn day, making chalk drawings on the sidewalk. I also see Andrew, the community complainer, but a very nice and sociable guy. A few other people are outside chatting, but I don't know their names.

After parking, I sit inside and let out a big sigh. Trying to prep my mind and body for climbing three flights of stairs. My apartment window looms above like I have to climb heaven to get there. I open the truck door and slide slowly out of the seat. Everyone knows what I do for a living. They basically let me be, so no worries about questions as to why I'm limping or having a bad hair day, so to speak.

"Hi Mr. Cocamoe." the children said, stopping their drawing as I limp up on the sidewalk.

"Hey Lil' ones."

Carlito waves. I give him a head nod as the others casually wave to me.

I'm nearer to my building, cussing and fussing to myself about what idiot designed it. A second-floor apartment, where you have to walk up three stupid ass flights to get there, major design flaw to me. Getting more pissed limping to these steps, I stop. I'm thinking about asking one of the guys talking out front for a little help, but I don't. My next step forward is very odd, any pain I had is gone. No pain in stump, arm, ribs or chest; my body is straightening out. Weird. Very weird, but I'll take it.

Just then, I thought about going to check my mailbox. It's only ten feet or so away from where I am, but don't want to chance the pain coming back. I go up the steps quickly, all three flights proving to be no problem, surprisingly. At the top landing, I unlock my door entering fast, closing the door behind me faster. My apartment's in pretty much the same condition I left it in, but why wouldn't it be. Guess I was hoping all of today's crap was a dream. I remove the scrub shirt easily, throwing it onto the floor, next to the table in the kitchen/dining room, was aiming for the chair. Walking past the kitchen/dining room, I press the answering machine button on the phone on the hallway desk. There are ten messages.

"Asshole, don't forget to take your meds, I called your cell but got no answer." Message one, from April.

Message two, April,

"Look, I want you to get some rest and sleep. I want you to remember our argument, I'd come over today but I don't want to see you."

Message three, April,

"Are you sleep or just ignoring me? I called your cell again assho…."

I press erase, the next six messages were her as well; her phone number shows in the message board window, I erased them too. They were probably all hang-ups anyway. The last message is from Shaun.

"Hope you're feeling better and you made it home ok, even though you're a jerk. Hey, you think April can put in a good word for me with the vampire nurse?"

Smiling as that message plays, I'm on the edge of my bed now, slowly taking off my pants, then my prosthetic leg. Not a big fan of wheelchairs, so I usually keep my leg on until I'm ready to go to sleep, like right now.

Laying down on my bed, I begin to feel warm and agitated. Even though I'm shirtless, I begin sweating a lot through the wrap.

"Damn!"

I sit up looking at my window. It's closed and the damned screen isn't installed. I just undid myself. Thought about snatching my leg to put it back on, instead I stand, grabbing hold of my bed's headboard. Balancing myself with the wall, nightstand and dresser, I hop over to open the window. The breeze feels great, as I stand there staring out into the woods behind my complex, just looking-not really thinking, just looking. I should install the screen, but I'd rather lay down.

Halfway back to the bed, my stomach gets nauseous fast. I rush to get to my bed. On my nightstand are the meds I got from the hospital. Not bothering to see what they're actually for, I pop 5 down my throat without water. A nasty, dry taste. Easing fully down onto the bed, today's events go through my head again, when eventually, I doze off.

"Ahhhh, Shit!"

Torturous pain wakes me and I glance quickly at my clock. I see that it's 3:11 a.m. before sweat blurs my vision. My stomach's twisting inside unmercifully. There's intense throbbing pain in my right stump. I've had phantom pain before, but not like this. I stretch my amputated leg out, trying to get relief, but it only gets worse. My whole body is in pain now and on fire.

"What the fuck is going on?"

My body rocks back and forth, sideways, then all directions. I'm a mere puppet to this pain. Sweat bursts from my entire body while I clutch the headboard and the side of the bed, straining to withstand this agony. My stump begins to sting and pulsate even deeper. Horror becomes more evident as I watch the veins in my stump start moving, swirling around, rapidly crashing into one another. It feels like my stump's going to burst wide open. My hell gets worse when it actually does.

"OH MY GOD!"

Joe Cocamoe's stump explodes open. A femur thrusts through, taking the place of the emptiness. Cocamoe tries pulling back his hand, but can't. Horrifyingly, he's witnessing a sinful, hostile takeover. Both arms and legs pulsate, growing and distorting into elongated limbs with long extended claws at the ends. The amputated limb is now fully grown as blood and other secretions drip onto the bed. Coarse dark hair begins to push out of all parts of his enlarging body. Cocamoe, wide-eyed, convulses wildly, causing the bed to violently jerk across the carpeted floor. He falls to the floor onto his left side; his now animal-like limbs flailing violently into the air; clawing and fighting with God. April's hospital wrap encasing his chest blasts off the growing (increasingly) deforming shell.

His face protracts outward violently, stretching and growing with the same coarse dark fur encasing his body. Loud excruciating grunts and cries are replaced by deep and uncivil low growls. Long sharp canine teeth strain their way out its elongated snout. Cocamoe grows into his now hideous self, a Werewolf.

The beast gazes at itself in the full-length mirror on the bedroom door. Its attention to itself is taken away by the sound of loud banging coming from the floor below. Arching its back, the werewolf looks in the direction of the noise, hearing,

"Keep it down up there! What the hell are you doing!" Andrew, the downstairs neighbor shouts, causing the werewolf to raise its head, snarling.

It turns its head to the fully open screenless window. In an instant, it jumps out of the window. Landing effortlessly and silently onto the ground, it takes off into the woods behind the apartment complex. In a vigorous trot, the werewolf surveys its surroundings. Taking in every sound, smell and sight within the woods, it's hunger and thirst for a meal is smelled not too far away. The werewolf's pace slows into a crouching leering stalk. Up ahead in a clearing, is a lone deer grazing. Crouching lower and cautiously, the werewolf's only thought is to eat. Suddenly, the deer looks up. Something has caught its attention and it bounds away fast, causing the werewolf to slink behind dense brush to see what's frightened its meal away.

Pulling into the area where the deer once was, is a car. Inside, an elderly couple; a man and a woman. The man is dying of stage 4 lung cancer and she's been a long-time sufferer of depression. They're smiling at one another as he stops the car. For a second, they sit there gazing at one another when they embrace and kiss. Upon releasing one another, the elderly man displays a small handgun. The elderly woman smiles again, extending her hand to support his holding the gun.

While the couple reassures themselves that their planned murder-suicide is right, the werewolf has moved closer to the passenger side of the car. The elderly man exhales deeply before kissing the elderly woman again. Leaning back, he raises the gun pointing it at his elderly female partner. Preparing himself physically and mentally for the task. She faces him, eyes closed; waiting for the impact of the bullet, desperately trying to remember them as they once were.

Crudely, the car passenger window explodes into a new hell neither is prepared for. Two gruesome long hairy arms wrangle the front of the elderly woman's neck, ripping it open, spraying the elderly man with the blood and pieces of the elderly woman. This is followed fiercely by the face of what could be the devil himself, embedding teeth into the rear of her neck. The sound of her crunching and bursting bones would've drowned out the elderly man's screams if horror had not silenced him.

Her floundering arms hit the elderly man's hand holding the gun, causing it to discharge twice. One bullet catches her in her left eye, mixing her fresh blood with the nauseating stench of the werewolf's mouth. The other bullet pierces the unsightly bloody paw of the werewolf. It flinches, continuing to eat. With its other paw, the werewolf grabs the head of the elderly man and pulls him closer. In that same motion, it releases the rear of the elderly woman's neck and engulfs the entire head of the already dead elderly man, heart failure his lucky demise.

The werewolf climbs fully inside the car, jostling it with its excessive weight, to resume its feral attack. Staining the interior of the car red, black and the colors of the elderly couple's last meal. The miasma of death filters from the car, along with the werewolf's triumphant howl, warning and announcing horrors yet to come.

After its feeding, the werewolf crawls out of the car, drenched in blood, human juices and pieces. Water and rest are it's cravings now. Slowly sniffing the crisp cool night, it detects the smell of water in the distance, thus beginning its journey to quenching another thirst.

A few hundred yards into its lope through Seawell State Park, the werewolf comes upon the decomposing body of a human not far from a narrowing end of a gully. It's the one who put him in his current state. Stopping, it gets closer to the rotting body, sniffing it.

In an appearance of reverence, the werewolf raises its head, howling a ghastly howl of praise.

Its fervent quest for water proceeds. Within a few minutes, the werewolf is at the edge of a stream in the park. Ambling closer to the water, it briefly looks at its reflection, then drinks; subsequently sinking into the bushes to rest.

4 MISSING LEG

I hear music, very loud music. My neighbor is going to get his ass kicked. I'm thinking to myself.

Rising up, I realize I'm neither in my bed nor my damned apartment. Trees, grass, leaves, and bushes surround me. I hear people, many people, sounding as if I'm in a concert hall with their voices echoing loudly, running one into another. I quickly throw my hands over my ears when all of a sudden my nose is force-fed smells from all over, attacking me. Wide-eyed, I'm looking in all directions trying to figure out what the hell is going on.

"Oh, shit, what the fuck is this?"

Springing back, from where I lay, I see blood on the grass, my arms, my chest, and leg.

"I'm bleeding .....!?"

Hysterically checking myself for wounds, I realize I'm also naked. There also a large hole partially healed on my right hand. It wasn't there when I went to bed. My head is spinning. I'm not remembering a damned thing. In my delirium, I try to get up but instead fall face first into a long narrow ass stream.

"Water! What the.....? Oh, shit, where the hell is my fucking leg?"

I start searching this small area for my prosthetic leg, crawling around on my hands and knees, but it's not here. Those earlier sounds and smells dissipated, now I begin hearing sirens in the distance. Looking up, I still only see fucking trees. The sirens seem further away. Hurriedly, I start washing blood off myself by throwing water on my naked body from the stream. It's too narrow to throw my 6 foot 3-inch frame into, even without the damned leg.

After my quick wash, I need to find out where I am and what the hell happened. Crawling to the bushes to take a peek out, I see several people jogging by. I'm surprised no one heard me screaming earlier. There are new sounds I hear now. Sneakers hitting the ground, the fabric of sweat suits brushing against skin, people talking far off, and still sirens in the distance. Somehow the noises and smells aren't as intense as before. It's like my body adjusted or something. Weird, very weird. Have to think and think quickly.

I see a guy jogging alone, slowly coming my way. My first intention is to yell out to him that I need help, but he has earbuds in his ears and the music is loud. Every instrument in the song he's listening to rocks my head into slight delirium. I've got to do something drastic to get his attention.

"Help! I've been robbed, please help me, please help!" I scream, falling out of the bushes, scaring the shit out of him.

I see him jump back, assuming a martial arts defensive stance. Even from my awkward position of trying to cover my penis with one hand, and my other hand propping myself up off the ground, I know he's prone for the attack. I guess seeing how shameful my naked-ass looks changes his look of fear into a new one named pity.

Lowering his hands, he also lowers the volume. The lone jogger searches his surroundings trying to get a better understanding of what the hell he's encountered. Time for me to go for the Oscar performance.

"Sir, please help me. I was attacked by several punks. I'm a federal officer working undercover. They took my prosthetic leg and my clothes. Call Detective Norris at Northwest Police District, my name is Agent Joseph Cocamoe."

My mind races, Detective Norris's name came out of the blue. Still somewhat guarded, the jogger cautiously takes off his jacket and removes his towel from around his neck, handing them to me to cover myself. Next, he helps me sit up so I can lean against a tree. He pulls out his cell phone dialing the operator to get a connection to the Northwest Police District. Once connected, he asked for Detective Norris, telling the dispatcher that Federal Agent Joseph Cocomoe requests him at Seawell State Park. The jogger tells her to 'hold on'. He gets silent as he moves the phone away from his face with this puzzled look.

"Excuse me, sir, they say Detective Norris is here at the park now."

I knew that I heard the dispatcher on the other end say that, but I didn't say anything to him. Hell, he's nervous enough and still doubtful of my requests or actions.

"He is? Can you give them our location and have him come here quick."

He shakes his head 'yes'.

"I'm sorry, I'm back. This Federal Agent is disabled, he's been robbed and there's a situation with his clothes and his leg,....they took them. His clothes and his leg. Yeah, I said he's nude and they took his prosthetic leg. His name again is Agent Joseph Cocamoe. Yes, he's asking specifically for Detective Norris. Yes, ok, thank you. We're by the bridge overpass at the edge of the stream on Leakin Drive. Yes, I have on a red t-shirt and black shorts. I'll stay with the Agent. My name? Herman Taylor."

As Mr. Taylor talks to the dispatcher, I'm looking around trying to piece together shit from last night to right now with no luck.

"Sir, they are notifying Detective Norris now."

"Thank you, Mr. Taylor, is it?"

"Yes, Herman Taylor."

"My name is, oh yeah you already know my name. I really appreciate your help."

"Is there anything I can get you…."

"No. I know this is really, really awkward. Naked one-legged man jumps out of the bushes in front of you, messing up your jogging routine and shit. A real screwed up day for many people. Can you tell me what time it is?" I said, positioning myself better against the tree.

"Sure, 7:25 a.m.."

I hear a car coming up behind us in the distance. Turning, I see it's a Seawell State Park police car. A Park Ranger gets out, approaching us calmly.

"Good morning, gentlemen. I'm Park Ranger Calvin. What seems to be the trouble here?" he said, slowly assessing both me and Mr. Taylor.

For some odd reason, I became belligerent and angry.

"We're here taking in some goddamn sun, what the fuck you think is going on here?"

Both Herman Taylor and Ranger Calvin's faces registered shock at what my response; I, too, was kind of surprised.

"Sir there's no need for that type of talk. I want to see some identification now!" Ranger Calvin bellows, becoming more assertive and direct.

Mr. Taylor reaches slowly into his shorts pocket producing his wallet, whereas I just sit there, reeling mentally from all the shit going on. Ranger Calvin finishes checking over Mr. Taylor's ID, then approaches me.

"I'm sorry for that outburst, Ranger. As you can see, I have no wallet or pants." I said, looking at the uncertainty in his, and the jogger's faces. I really was sorry for what I said.

Ranger Calvin looks at me then turns away, walking to the rear of his car. He opens the trunk, coming back with a pair of Seawell State Park Police sweatpants and a t-shirt. Handing them to me, I position my body to put the pants on, then the t-shirt. Both men help me get up and escort me to the rear seat of the Park Ranger police car.

"Can you sit tight here for a few minutes? Get warm. I'd like to ask Mr. Taylor a few questions." Ranger Calvin demanded.

"Sure, no problem. Where am I going to go?"

Ranger Calvin closes the door but never turns on the car for me to get warm. Bastard. He walks Herman away from the car, turning his back to me in the process. As I sit, I again try to figure out what happened to me, and how I got like this, when I can hear the conversation between the two men. They are approximately fifteen to twenty feet away and the car window is up, yet I hear them like they're in the car with me.

"So, Mr. Taylor, you said Mr. Cocamoe fell out of those bushes, naked, and reported being a Federal Agent, who was robbed of clothing and his leg, correct?"

"Yes sir, that's what he said happened."

"Really? Did you see or notice anything strange other than what you stated?"

"No. No sir."

"Thank you, sir. Would you mind staying right here please?"

Adjusting myself in preparation for his questions, my thoughts are interrupted by another noise, a car I hear coming pretty fast up the road. Somehow, I can sense that the car is a mile away and it has the distinct smell of strawberry jelly.

Moments later, an unmarked police car pulls up on the passenger side of the Park Ranger car. It's Detective Norris. Ranger Calvin goes to greet him.

"Good morning. I'm Park Ranger Calvin. May I help you?"

"I'm Detective Norris, from Northwest," Norris said, displaying his ID.

"I have a victim in the rear of my car and the gentleman standing over there is the one that called the incident in." Ranger Calvin said.

Detective Norris looks around the area slowly, looks in the rear of the Park Ranger car at me, then turns back to Ranger Calvin.

"Thank you, Ranger Calvin, for your help, your services are no longer needed. I hope you got a full statement from that gentleman. You can get it to me at Northwest Police District. I'll transport Agent Cocamoe."

Detective Norris disposition is cold and silent as he opens the Park Ranger car door. I attempt to say 'hi' but he quickly grabs my left arm and pulls me out, almost having us both fall to the ground. Luckily Ranger Calvin, still miffed at Norris's chilly actions, catches us.

"Dude, what's the hurry? I was real comfy. To think I specifically asked for your ass."

Norris, without the help of Ranger Calvin, gets me into the rear of his car. Not saying a single word to me, he jumps in the driver's seat and we pull off. My body lurches deep into the hard uncomfortable backrest of the leather seats. Detective Norris smirks, hearing me fumbling around for stability. Once situated, I sit up straight. There's no comfort level in this hard ass seat, but I do relax and take in the now morbid beauty of Seawell State Park.

Unexpectedly, a quick, tingling chill spiders down my spine, my back pushing heavily against these suck ass seats, while my left knee digs into Norris's driver's seat. No words from Norris, nor I to him.

Two miles into our drive, Norris slows the car and stops.

"Mr. Bounty Hunter, what time did your incident occur?"

"For real? I have no idea."

"Really? Can you tell me why you were in the park? When I saw you last you were claiming illness and were in a rush to get home?"

"Well Detective, the meds did put me out, then for some weird ass reason I woke up here, in the park, naked and legless."

Detective Norris doesn't reply, the look on his face made him seem like he was in deep thought. I decided to ask,

"Why were you already in the park this morning, what happened, you ate all your strawberry jelly and there's a sale here?"

"What? How'd you know I was already in the park? And what's this about strawberry jelly? Is it all over my face or something? You know, I can arrest you for impersonating a Federal Officer."

"Calm down gumshoe, technically I AM a Federal Officer...sort of. Never mind that, when the jogger, Mr. Taylor called your precinct, they told him you were already here. And the jelly, I smelled it on you a mile away."

"My damned department, too frickin' transparent! If arresting you on Federal charges wouldn't involve a bunch of peons, and cause me way too much paperwork, we'd be on our way to booking." He scoffs, looking at me strangely in the rear-view mirror, discreetly checking if he has jelly on his face or clothing.

"So, you gonna tell me why you're here, or what?" I asked.

"Police business!" Norris yells.

"Well, who's to say the person who attacked me didn't do what you came here to investigate."

"I doubt it."

"Look, you're here for a damned good reason. Why so hush-hush? How do you know they ain't related?"

"You'd be dead right now. That's how I know."

"Dead? So homicide is why you're here Detective? Ok, let's say your perp got to your person first. They were easy pickings, so they killed them. When he, or they, got to me, they felt challenged and something stopped them from killing me. Even though I'm just guessing."

"Continue guessing, leave real police work to me. But if you really must know, two people, we think, a man and a woman, were mutilated and killed."

"Two people? You think. Really? Why do you just 'think' two people?" I said.

"Bodies are too mangled to really tell if it's one or more."

I start wondering if that thing that attacked me the other day was still out there. I also wonder if I should come clean with Detective Norris and tell him about what happened to me the other night. Maybe if I do, it'll help get that thing captured. No. He won't believe me. Maybe I can take him to The Store and Derek can corroborate my story by saying his client Randy was half eaten. Better yet, Shaun is Norris's cousin and he'll tell the truth. Hell no, hell no! Then I'd have to come clean with Shaun, AND April. I'll just let this one play itself out.

"Hey Bounty guy, you still have no idea who attacked you, took your clothes and your leg?"

"Once again, NO!"

"I find it difficult to believe a seasoned war vet, Army Ranger turned Bounty Hunter, got jumped, robbed of clothes and your leg, in the park at night and not remember any of it."

"Look, a lot of shit has me stumped too? I really hope you're taking me home now?"

"Home? That's where you were going when you almost crashed into me the other night. You said you were coming straight from the hospital. I checked, and you were there. You also said the meds were making you drowsy, what meds were you taking and what were they for? Did you take anything else, anything stronger? The bandages and wrappings you had, where are they? I guess they got stolen too?"

"Real funny. You didn't bother to find out why I was there I see. I was snuck by one of my client's homeboys, and the meds were for the pain and soreness I got from the beat down I gave him. And no, I didn't take anything else or anything stronger. The wrappings and bandages, no idea where they are."

"You mean to tell me you got your ass kicked twice in two days?"

"Once, dammit. The earlier one got..."

"Got what?"

"Nothing. I'm pleading the fifth right now. Just take me home." I said, looking out the side window thinking about that wolf-thing and the situation I'm in now.

After a moment of silence, Norris speaks,

"Fine. I'll take you home but my questioning isn't over. I can wait till you get your mouthpiece. No problem."

Funny, he's assuming I want a lawyer. I just want to stop answering his stupid ass questions and go home.

"Can you undo the fifth and tell me where you live?"

I say nothing.

"I don't know where you live. You know that right?"

"Use your computer then."

Detective Norris looks in the rear view mirror, grunts then picks up the receiver to his police radio. He gives the dispatcher my full name and asks for my address, to which she obliges. Again, my mind is going through a thousand scenarios on how I ended up in the park like this and who did this to me, when my thoughts are jarred. Norris turns on the police car lights, throws the car in drive and the siren blares.

"Another issue to deal with. Got to get you home quick."

Those few miles to my apartment are loud and fast. As we pull into the gated front entrance of my complex, my neighbors scurry away to the insides of their units, away from unmarked police with lights flashing all ass-early in the morning.

Norris pulls in front of my building and sits there, not moving. He turns to me only because I'm not moving either.

'Oh, yeah. I forgot." Norris said, getting up out of the front seat to open the rear door.

Rear doors on police cars don't open from the inside. Plus, I'll need his help anyway getting to my apartment and he knows that.

I slide myself to the edge of the seat. As he leans down I take hold of his shoulder. Norris is a few inches shorter than me so he's basically the perfect crutch. I hold on to him as I hop toward my building. Of course, all are watching without being seen.

"Do you have a wheelchair?" Norris asked.

"Nope, they slow me down. Just get me to the steps and you can go handle your police business."

As we got to the bottom of the first flight of steps, an apartment door near the mailboxes opens up.

"I'll help him up the steps officer." Carlito blurts out.

Without hesitation, Norris hands me over to him and heads back to his car.

"Don't leave town, Cocamoe!" Norris shouts.

Carlito, measuring out the logistics of helping me, shows his dismay of police as Norris pulls off. Since he and I are the same height, he stays one step below to give me leverage. There's silence on the way up until we reach the top of level one.

"You know you don't have to do this," I said.

Carlito smiles as we continue on to the second flight when another apartment door opens. This time, it's Andrew, who lives in the unit below mine. He's also the one that complains about everything; noise, parties, trash, pets, kids, air... you name it.

"Yes?" Carlito and I say in unison, annoyed that he's appeared.

"Damn neighbors. I just came out to help. If I don't, Y'all be all day getting up these steps."

Andrew, walks to the side of me, opposite Carlito, staring at my outfit.

"What's up with these tight ass sweats?"

"Don't worry about that. So, you two going to carry me up two flights. Andrew, you sure you can do that. I know Carlito works out but dude, you're scrawny."

With me saying that Andrew lifts me up under my left leg and we're on our way.

"Whoa partner," I said, grabbing tighter to them both, maintaining my balance.

Getting me to my apartment door in one piece, I place my leg firmly onto the ground and reach for keys I don't have. Carlito, noticing I have no keys, pulls out his wallet. He looks at my door handle, whips out a credit card and unlocks my door. Good thing I only locked the bottom lock.

"I'm going to act like I didn't see that!" Andrew scoffs.

"You need help once you're in or what?" Carlito asks, ignoring Andrew.

"No. I got it. I just want to lay down, thanks, guys."

"Cool. No problem homes." Carlito said.

"Yeah. Whatever." Andrew mumbles.

Thanking them again before closing my door, I hear them arguing going down the stairs. Finally, I'm in my apartment. Relieved, but there's a real funky smell coming from somewhere in this place. Probably something in the garbage disposal. Too tired and bummed out to worry about it, I grab hold of the end of the small table by the front door. It's not far from a medium height stool with wheels. To get to the stool, I release my grip on the small table and plant my face, chest, and thighs against the wall. Slowly moving my foot by turning it in, then out, staying connected to the wall. I'm much too tired to do the hopping routine I did last night in my bedroom.

Standing next to the stool, positioning my ass perfectly, I drop onto it. I extend my left leg to grab the edge of the wall, to keep from rolling, and my right arm down to get my balance. Securing myself on the stool, I roll towards my hall closet where my spare prosthetic is. While rolling, I see my main prosthetic, against the bed. Right where I left it, last night when I took it off.

"What the fuck is going on here?"

I reach for that leg, but the smell, stronger here, almost keeps me out. Picking it up, I cover my nose taking a look around the bedroom for clues or signs that would help me understand what's going on.

The bedroom window is still open. That, I remember. Meds and cell on the nightstand, check. No screen in the window; I remember that, too. Turning around doing further checking, I see blood and all kinds of other crap splattered on my bed, wall, floor, and ceiling. My t-shirt and hospital wrappings are shredded to pieces on the floor, along with stuff that looks like hair. NONE of this shit do I remember.

"Someone's playing with my fucking head and I don't like it. Who'd do some crazy shit like this to me?"

Then it hits me.

"Derek!"

His ass is the only one who could do some shit like this to me and try to get away with it. Then I think, maybe Shaun. Naw, he'd be too afraid of what I'd do to him.

In grabbing my cell to dial Derek, I move my hand away from my nose. The smells, for some probably real fucked up reason, are tolerable now.

The cell connects.

"Yo, what up?" Derek asks.

"Motherfucker, I know it was you who drugged me somehow. Pulled me out of my bed naked and legless. Then splattered blood and shit on my walls and left me out in the woods last night!"

"I don't like your damned tone you Army Ranger fuck. First off, what the hell are you talking about? Me drugging you and getting your dumb ass out of the bed naked with no leg? What was the other thing? Oh yeah, leaving you in the woods and splattering blood in your apartment. Ha, Ha, Ha. That shit's funny, but no, dude, I didn't do that. I kinda wish I had. My ass is in Reno. Been here since after you and Shaun dropped off puzzle boy Randy!"

"Reno, Nevada, for real? So if you didn't do this shit, then who?"

"Dude, no clue. You might not want to mention this story to anyone else. So, we done here, or what?"

"Man don't lie to me. Tell me you did this shit!" I yell, almost pleading.

"Sorry dude, really. I've been in Nevada for the last 15 hours. You might wanna go see a doctor, Cocamoe."

"Yeah, yeah. My bad. Saw a doc, meds, and weed don't mix. Sorry to bother you."

Getting more confused made me madder and feeling a lot more stupid.

"Hey, I'll be back tomorrow. Get some rest dumb-fuck then come by The Store 'round 2:30 p.m. I may have a client for you. If you're up to it, that is." Derek said.

"Yeah, tomorrow, 2:30 p.m., ok bye," I said, disconnecting the call.

I glance at the cell thinking I should call Shaun or April. The thought left quickly with me yawning and stretching, feeling a slight soreness in my stump. I'm still on the stool. In order for me to lay down, I need to transfer to my bed. These nasty ass sheets need to go first. I yank them off my bed, rolling them into a ball and sling them onto the floor. I'll deal with them and the other crap tomorrow. Going to get some sleep. To be on the safe side, I'm sleeping with my 9mm and my knife.

5 THE VISITOR

Night eases by smoothly, like a pickpocket at Mardi Gras, putting me to sleep. An ignorant loud knock on my damned front door wakes me. Holding my gun tightly, I roll my eyes to my nightstand to check the time, the clock reads 6:45 a.m. Whoever it is, fucking knocks again.

"Who the fuck is it!"

"Dude, it's me. I was in the neighborhood so I'm here to check on you!!" Shaun yells.

"Shit. Man, I'm ok; it's too early for this crap, go away!"

Shaun knocks again.

"Dammit, Shaun! Hold on!"

Placing gun and knife down on the bed, I throw on a pair of boxers I get from my nightstand drawer and connect my good prosthetic leg to my stump. Once connected, I mosey to the front door with my weapons. To be sure, I look out the peephole.

"Why, Shaun? Why? Do you know what time it is?" I said, opening the door.

He hurries in, passing me.

"Close the door, man, close the door," Shaun said, going straight to my fridge, pulling it open, searching, then finding one of my brews.

"Shaun, be for real. You weren't in the neighborhood; you live on the other side of the city. So, why are you here?"

"Damn dude. I was in your hood. Just didn't expect to leave it like this."

"What are you talking about?"

I look back out the peephole when I hear people running down the steps. Shaun jumps to the side of the refrigerator.

"Who's that?" he asks, trying to hide.

"I don't know. They kept on running. What the hell did you do?"

"Man, I didn't know."

"Didn't know what?"

"You know, the vampire nurse, from the hospital. Well, she lives three buildings up from you, with her husband. We were grooving all night. I woke up early, still trying to groove. She was into to it too, until we hear keys at the front door and she freaks out. I hear her mumbling something like 'he's supposed to be gone for a week'. Then I hear her clearly when she says for me to get my shit and go out the sliding glass door."

Laughing at Shaun, I open my fridge for the other beer.

"I had no idea she was married. Next thing I know, my naked ass is being pushed off the second-floor balcony with my clothes and shoes following."

"Serves your ass right. You need to chill on your womanizing." I said, walking back into my bedroom, feeling both relieved, and confused. Shaun was too occupied with getting at Sara for the last few days, so I know he couldn't have taken me and left me in the woods that night.

"There's a lot of nakedness going on around this complex," I said.

Shaun, is right behind me, following me to my bedroom.

"So, what we doing today boss? And what's that damned smell?"

"We? My ass is going back to sleep. Waking up at around noon, getting some grub then going to The Store. You are either going to go home or take your ass back up to the front and crash on the sofa. The smell, that's my bouts with gas, something I ate."

Shaun's still walking behind me. I turn around facing him with a gun in one hand, the beer in the other and knife in my boxer waistband. Turning away from me fast reaches in the bathroom grabbing my air freshener. He sprays it several times before running to the front and throwing himself onto the sofa.

His spraying mixes with the funk badly, pissing me off. Wired and mad as shit, I go into the bathroom to get my big ass metal bucket inside the tub. I start filling it with water while gathering my sponge mop, spray bottle with lemon juice, hydrogen peroxide and three rolls of paper towels under the sink.

Going back into my bedroom with my cleaning shit, I slam the door, prepped for a quick clean up. First, I spray the walls and ceiling with my lemon juice spray bottle and hydrogen peroxide. Next, the wet sponge mop. Squeegeeing the wall and parts of the ceiling loosens the blood and other crap. It's coming out, not as noticeable and the smell is dissipating. Afterward I spray the lemon juice, mixed with water, onto my carpet and the bed coverings on the floor. My attempts to scrub away with a sponge mop on a carpeted floor is a bad idea. It's almost working, acting like a scrub brush, but not quite.

Without warning, flashes of that thing attacking me, Randy getting mutilated, my being in the woods naked and legless are back. Something's really fucked up. I have no idea what or why.

"I can't do this shit!" I shouted, kicking the bed coverings, lemon bottle, hydrogen peroxide, and unopened paper towels hard into one of the corners of my bedroom.

"Dude! You ok in there!" Shaun yells, knocking on my door.

"Yeah. Go back up front, I'm cool." I said, picking up the bucket with the sponge mop still inside and place it on top of the bed coverings and cleaning crap.

"You sure man sounds like you're fighting your room."

"It won. Go back up front Shaun."

"Alright. Your crib dude," he said, shuffling back up front, flopping back on the sofa.

My bedroom walls and ceiling are dripping, a clean lemony dripping, when I hear cartoons from the front room. Shit, now I don't feel like staying here. I put on some sweatpants, my own this time and a black Henley. Grabbing my jacket and holster, I hurry out my bedroom.

"Shaun, let's go," I said, rushing by him opening my front door.

I didn't look for his reaction, just needed to hear him moving.

"Crazy asshole. Fights his bedroom, farts all over the place, sprays too much of that lemon shit in his bedroom, now he wants to leave 7:30 in the morning." Shaun said, under his breath.

I'm already on the second flight of stairs when I see Shaun being hesitant coming out of the front door of my apartment.

"Come on, there's no one out here," I shout.

Shutting my door, Shaun runs down to catch up.

"Where we going?" he asked.

"Don't know. Just get in."

Shaun's truck is parked next to mine. I watch as he opens his door to get in. He stops when he sees me looking at him in disbelief as I stand by my truck.

"Fine, I'll get into yours," I said.

"Hey, you were walking normal. What's the name of those meds, I may need some later?" Shaun said, wiping a dirt spot off his truck.

"Don't know," I said, shaking my head.

"You know I don't want to leave my baby here. Unfamiliar truck, people see it, you know, vandalism and shit."

"I'm driving your truck, Shaun."

We switch places without any objection. Starting the engine and placing Shaun's truck in drive, I have no idea where we're going. At the last moment, I make a right turn leaving the apartment complex to go to the part of the park where I was found. I may find something there that the police could've missed.

During the drive there, I'm thinking hard about telling Shaun about what really happened to me the night I got Randy, and my nude incident at the park. Honestly should tell him, for his own safety. No telling if and when that wolf-thing I thought I killed will show up again. I'd better tell him, now.

"Shaun."

"Yeah, dude."

"I've got something to tell you. It's going to sound weird and unbelievable so hear me out."

"Does it have anything to do with that ugly ass mark on your right hand?"

I glance at my right hand.

"Oh, that. No. Don't know how that got there."

"Yeah, ok 'cause that wasn't there yesterday Cocamoe, remember I'm very observant dammit."

"Whatever, Shaun. Listen to me."

Shaun sits there waiting for my spiel. I tap my fingers slowly on the steering wheel, then it comes out.

"That night I tracked Randy, something very crazy and strange happened."

"Yeah, I know."

"No. No, you don't. Listen, really listen. That night, there was another one there. I told you and everyone else it was Randy's partner. Well, it wasn't. It was…It was a very large big ass wolf. A big fucking wolf that killed and ate Randy then attacked me. I fought it off, shot and stabbed it many times, it bit me, then……" I said, really not sure of what was coming out of my mouth or if it was understandable.

"Then what?" Shaun asked, with a slight smirk on his face.

"Fuck you, Shaun, you're not taking me seriously. Just forget I said any damned thing!"

"Naw dude, for real, my fault. What happened next?"

"That's ok. I knew I shouldn't say shit. Just fuck it."

"Cocamoe, serious bidness man, I'm listening. Come on dude, tell me what happened next."

After a few seconds of his begging, I give in. Telling the rest of the story.

"The wolf turned into a man!"

There are a few seconds of quiet heavy silence.

"A wolf, a big fucking wolf, ate Randy. Almost ate you. You fought it off, it bit you. You killed it. Then it turned into a man. Right?"

"Yeah, I know, you don't believe me."

"Believable doesn't even describe what you just told me. What kind of weed you been doing lately?"

"Fuck it!"

"Dude, hold up. I'm just messing with you. Truth is, I kind of believe you. I've known you over eight years, we've been through a lot of shit together, and you've never lied to me."

"Well, it is a story that's hard to believe. Still very hard for me to believe, but I was there, felt it and saw it."

"A wolf man huh? You tell April?"

"Hell no, it was hard enough telling your ass."

"So let's think about this. Wolf kills Randy, attacks you, bites you, you kill it, and it turns into a man. Mmmm….well if that wolf turned into a man, like you said, after you killed him, then that would make him a werewolf."

"A what?" I said, laughing lightly.

"It's not funny Cocamoe. A Werewolf, scary movie, wolfs-bane, silver bullet type shit."

"Werewolf? Real funny, no such thing. Maybe it was just one big hairy ass, crazy motherfucker."

Now, after what Shaun had just said, there are more doubts running through my head. I'm definitely not going to tell him I was naked and legless in the park the following day. Especially not after his 'werewolf' remark.

"Yup. One big crazy ass, hairy, stinky, non-showering motherfucker." Shaun said, looking at me, holding his nose in mock directed at me.

"Stinky? Hell, I think my smell is very appropriate, considering the shit I've been through. Why I gotta be fresh and clean around your ass anyway?"

"It's your body, or what used to be your body."

"Shut up. We're here."

"Here? Where is here?" Shaun asked, looking around.

"I want to check out this crime scene for a few minutes."

There's police tape in a number of places, but the area I want to check is behind the bushes I jumped out of.

"What are we looking for?" Shaun asked.

"Watch out for Park Rangers or police. Warn me if any show up." I said, quickly.

"I'm the damned lookout now?"

"C'mon, give me a damned break!" I said, fighting through the first set of bushes.

I make it to an area where the grass is slightly matted and everything around, well just smells familiar. This is where I was, I'm sure of it. Looking around though, there's nothing significant that jogs my memory about what happened before I woke up. Not even the blood on the ground. My tweezers and small plastic bag come in handy as I kneel down to get a sample. I need to know whose blood this is.

Police probably took samples of this grass and maybe even some water samples that may have had blood in it. Whoever this blood belongs to, they'll connect it and start looking for me. I hope there's no connection to the murders Detective Norris told me about in the park that night and this blood.

"Fuck! Not now." I grumble, straightening up fast from getting the blood sample because I hear Shaun and other voices loud and clear.

I turn to face them, but I'm still alone at the matted grass blood site. Forcefully, smells that weren't there before are with me. Vintage stale cologne, watered down perfume, roast beef, wine, cabbage, and gunpowder. This barrage to my senses has my head ringing and body shivering. I'm trying to get a grasp on how this comes and goes without warning, then leaves without saying 'goodbye'. Now, I only hear Shaun, talking to himself,

"If that thing was a werewolf, and it bit Cocamoe, then he's a werewolf too. I sure hope not, 'cause that'll be fucked up for real."

With hearing that, my composure, what's left of it, comes back. I walk back through the bushes to Shaun, thinking heavily about what he said both times about werewolves. The fact that I'm smelling and hearing like a dog does not help. Faintly, I feel my cell phone buzz in my pants pocket. Great, I need something to pull me away from my crazy thoughts. It's April.

"Hi, baby." I quietly said.

"Hi baby my ass. Where are you? I came past your apartment but you weren't there!"

"I'm sorry; it's been real crazy and busy. Shaun and I had to do some investigative work in Seawell."

"Shaun! You're with slutty ass, Shaun! I know about his rendezvous with Sara!"

Instantly, I defend Shaun.

"Slutty Shaun! What about slutty Sara, he didn't know she was married. Look I've got to go. Talk to you later!"

I'm within earshot of Shaun. He heard my conversation with April.

"That's April, right? I'm not a slut, no disrespect, but to hell with her!"

"You ARE a slut."

Before I open the truck's door, I look Shaun straight in his face.

"Another thing. I'm not a werewolf, so stop saying that shit."

Shaun looks at me, turns in the direction of the bushes that I just came from then turns to me again with his left eyebrow cocked upward. I get in the truck, but as usual, Shaun has to have the last word.

"Regardless of what you say, legend says, if a werewolf bites you, your ass turns into a werewolf too. Silver bullets only hurt werewolves not kill it, you've got to cut off brain activity like shoot or stab it in the head or heart, hang it, behead it or fire his ass up with flames! You know they can change without a full moon. Hey, how'd you hear what I said when your ass was way over there?"

Can't take it anymore. Grabbing Shaun by his shirt collar, I pull him into the truck from the driver's side. With our faces inches apart, I smell his fear and secretions of urine in his pants (tough guy pees his pants? Gotta establish his intimidation somewhere, for him peeing himself to be believable).

"I AM NOT A FUCKING WEREWOLF!" I shout.

Shaun's trembles, too afraid to pull away from me so I release him. My non-stop glare into his fallen eyes has him quickly move away from me to stare out the window.

"I'm hungry. Let's eat." I sneer, starting the truck.

Thoughts of apologizing to Shaun came and went just like the other shit that 'comes and goes', so I said nothing. Just enjoying the quietness of the ride to our favorite dive to eat, Lloyd's.

"After we eat, we're going to The Store," I shout, parking the truck a block up from Lloyd's.

He's quiet and pensive until he gets out of the truck slamming the door shut.

"Get it off your chest now! You're not fucking up my eating!" I yell, moving fast across the front of the truck to confront him.

Shaun cowers, covering his head in defense. Stopping myself, I look how frightened he is. I stand over him and place my hand on his shoulder, gently.

"Get up man, let's eat."

Little did I know we attracted a small crowd of onlookers.

"There's nothing to see here. Just two hungry assholes joking around." I said, trying to sound jovial and shit.

I wrap my arm around Shaun going into Lloyd's. Opening the door, I spot an empty table, but my walk to it is altered. The powerful smell of scrapple, bacon, burnt coffee and fried eggs assault my nose. Jerking my head back, I cover my nose thinking that weird shit is coming back, but it doesn't, this time. Shaun, ignoring me, goes directly to the bathroom. I sit down, ignoring him too, tit for tat dammit. Kari, our regular waitress, comes over.

"Good day animal, what's the matter, something else stinks in here?" Kari asks, watching my nose twitching from these hard stringent smells.

Kari smiles, watching Shaun walk away. She's a beautiful thirty something red head with a great athletic body and deserves better than him. Her being on the swim team at Pye State University, during her undergraduate years kept her in great shape. She's now in grad school and one of Shaun's former lovers, so they say.

I noticed how every time we come into Lloyd's to eat, Kari goes to the jukebox and plays "Still in Love With You" by Thin Lizzy. Sade did an excellent version of it too, but it's not in the jukebox. Shaun's supposed to be 'mister goddamn observant'.

"Hi, Kari, you know I love the burning food smell of this joint. But today I have a challenge for Lloyd. A juicy hamburger. Rare." I said, slightly covering my nose now.

"Rare? You beautiful animal you." Kari coos.

Shaun joins me at the table.

"What about you tiger? Do you want anything different?"

"I'll have a chocolate shake and fries." Shaun snaps, pulling his chair out to sit.

"Oh. Your usual, big spender." Kari said, walking away from our table.

Shaun watches her sashay away. Cracks a smile, then wails into me.

"What's your damned problem? That shit in the truck and in front of Lloyd's was uncalled for. I think this job has gotten you all screwed up in the head. You're not right!"

"Forget it, Shaun. I'm hungry."

Breaking up our new 'love fest', Kari comes back with our order.(That was fast. Explain the time)

"Chocolate shake and fries sweetie, ketchup's on the table, but you already know that." Kari said, placing Shaun's order on the table harshly.

We both gaze up at Kari as she's now presenting my food.

"Here's your undead meat, animal." Kari said, playfully growling, gently placing my order on the table.

"Funny. You never ordered anything rare before. Red meat is bad for you, especially raw red meat." Shaun said.

I said nothing, already had the hunk of bloody meat in my hand, oozing out of the bun, running down my hands. I lick off the blood and juices slowly, biting into the burger hard again. Shaun turns his head in disgust, yet manages to ask me to pass him a fork.

Pulling the burger from my mouth shows blood and meat picnicking around my lips. The couple at the next table cringe. There are no utensils on our table. With small chunks of meat drop from my bottom lip, I reach over to an empty table to get a fork.

"Ouch!" I scream, spewing blood and meat onto the empty table as I drop the fork.

My fingers are slightly burned. How? Why?

Kari runs to my aid. Shaun sits there with a strange look on his face. That lovely cringing couple got up and left.

"What happened sweetie?" Kari asked.

"Nothing, that fork must've just come out of the dishwasher or something" I said.

"You ok?" Kari asked.

"Yeah, I'm good." I said, trying to figure out what just happened.

Kari pulls a clean fork from her apron and hands it to Shaun.

"Who eats fries with a stupid fork anyway? Cocamoe, you sure you're ok?" Kari asks.

"Yes."

The remainder of our lunch was uneventful. Shaun avoiding eye contact with me as he ate, (You said they got up and lefts. I'm asking for the check to pay the bill when my cell phone buzzes.

"What up." I said, removing lint off my phone case.

"You still coming by?" asked Derek.

"Yup, just finishing up lunch."

"Fine, see you in a few."

Shaun gets up from the table, thoughts of apologizing to him filter through, but I don't.

"That was Derek; he wants to know where we are." I said.

Shaun, walks past me to get to Kari. He hugs her tightly, then walks out of Lloyd's. I follow suit. While hugging Kari, I see Shaun outside on his cell. When I walk out of Lloyd's, I hear him quickly say "later" and he disconnects.

"Sara." he said.

He was lying; on the phone was his cousin, Detective Norris.

"Cool, let's roll." I said.

We get into the truck and start on our way to The Store when Shaun cell rings. He quickly answers it.

"What up cuz. Yeah, with him now. Going to see Derek......"

I snatch the phone from Shaun then drop it as my hand burns again, this time from Shaun's cell phone.

"Man fuck this!" Shaun yells, punching me in my right jaw.

He doesn't notice that the cell phone has burned my hand. More strange shit for me to think about. His punch though, causes me to swerve the truck to the left of the road, barely missing a yellow cab coming our way. I stop the truck in the middle of the road. Feeling another punch coming, I reach up grabbing his fist with my hand.

"Okay, okay. I get it man, I'm not me today. I'm not feeling right. I'm sorry. I'm sorry about all the shit I did today. For real man." I said, feeling really bad about all he and I have gone through in the last few hours.

Shaun relaxes his arm and his face, so I release his fist.

A few seconds pass.

"Why are we still sitting here? We got a gig to get to!" Shaun (oxymoron)We've had many fist fights before, all ending the same way. Acting like nothing ever happened, carrying on with what we need to do. He is my partner, and the brother I never had.

Straightening out the truck to go ahead, I take a look at my right palm. Two burn marks now, one from the fork, the other from the cell phone.

Shaun probably had the phone in the sun too long when I snatched it, although that doesn't make sense. Not going to dwell on it too much, lot's of shit going on lately doesn't make sense.

6 HASSAN

Making it to The Store, we walk right into Derek's stinky cigar smoke. There's more light and two desks are clear of everything. Where Derek sits remains a mess.

"Come in gentlemen, come in. I've got another runner. Name of Edgar Quali. Last time anyone's seen him was near 33rd and Greenmount."

"How much?" I ask.

"Only ten g's and your ass only gets ten percent dammit no matter what!" Derek said, handing me the fugitive sheet with Edgar's picture, aliases, height, weight and last known residences.

"Yeah, ten percent, got you." I said, giving a half salute, turning to leave.

"I want him alive. Shaun you're my damned witness. ALIVE! HEAR ME?" Derek screams.

"No problem, whole body, breathing, got it!" I yell, walking out of The Store.

On the sidewalk, Shaun takes the fugitive picture from my hand.

"Let's see what a thousand dollar fugitive looks like. Funny looking dude, ain't he?"

"Any who, we'll go this Saturday night. Mr. Edgar is into dog fighting and I hear on the street there's a big one that night on Barclay, around 1:00 a.m.." I said.

"You did, from who?" Shaun asks.

"Sources dude. Sources." I reply.

Little did he know that I heard about the dog fight while we were in Lloyd's. Still haven't figured out how and why, at times I can hear and smell like that. Thankfully, it's not all the time. Maybe I should go see Dr. Seti. Maybe when my head hit that boulder the other night it jarred something in my brain. I really just want to go back to my place and lay down and rest. Then I remember, today is Thursday. Every other Thursday night, myself,

April, Shaun and his catch of the day, go to Club 898 to get our party on. Perhaps going out will make me forget about all the craziness.

"Shaun, you drive, I'm tired. I need to rest up for tonight. You do remember, it's Thursday, Club 898." I said, throwing him the keys, to his truck.

"Yeah, I remember. You haven't patched things up with April yet so you sure we're going."

"In due time. She's probably at my crib waiting for her lover man, then off to the club we go." I said, grinning.

"Yeah, waiting to kill you."

"After she ravages my body with hers, she can kill me. " I said, buckling my seat belt, slinking into the seat to get some sort of shut-eye.

We were riding for about 20 minutes or so when I hear Shaun yell out,

"Ooohh, there's Hassan!"

Hassan is one of the few "Arabbers" left in Baltimore, a local street merchant, selling fruits vegetables, and other items from a horse drawn cart.

"Watermelon, collards, and good tasting stuff. Come get 'em now, makes life less rough!" Hassan chants his Arabbers tune.

Shaun slows the truck to park. At first I was a little pissed we were stopping but I hadn't seen Hassan in a while and I do need some apples. He's fun to talk to and some of the customers are leaving. Less hassles for me.

Hassan's older than Shaun, and I, 70 maybe 80 years old. According to Hassan himself, he's way over 100, with old ass stories to match. I love his 'old man' stories. Especially the one about him not being able to fight in the Mahdist War in the 1880's in Egypt. He says he was shot in the ass by a British soldier who caught him in a British General's wife's chambers. Supposedly, that's how he got his permanent limp.

When he saw us, his tight grizzled face lights up. I agree there are many years in his face but not over 100. I refuse to believe that, but who am I to discourage a cool old dude?

"Marshall Dillon" and "Festus", how you boys doing?" Hassan said, always referring to us as old TV show police characters.

Hassan corals Shaun, giving him a big hug. He does the same to me, but It's followed by a slow release and a critical stare. His nappy gray beard seems electrified on his dark, smooth, ebony skin, as his dark eyes display a sense of worry and pain, making me uncomfortable. I get more uncomfortable when Hassan's horse begins acting jittery pulling the cart forward, like it's trying to get away from something. Hassan steps away from me quickly, grabbing the reins, to calm his horse.

"What you need?" Hassan asked Shaun.

"Hook me up with a pound of collards, about five sweet potatoes, and half a pound of those red grapes." Shaun said.

With that, Hassan slaps the reins into Shaun's hand as he hurries to gather up his requested items. At the same time, Hassan's motioning for me to move across the street. Like a little kid I oblige him.

Feeling uneasy, I'm wanting to hear one of his impromptu stories, but he's busy getting Shaun's stuff.

"Hassan, how've you been? Haven't seen you in a minute!" I shout from across the street.

He just looks at me, mumbles something while weighing Shaun's collards. Funny, I didn't hear what he mumbled.

"Hmph....Oh well." I said to myself.

Once again, I try to strike up conversation with Hassan.

"You see the game the other night? I missed it all because my ass had to work."

Hassan doesn't respond as he packages up Shaun's goods pretty fast, for an old dude with a limp.

"No charge, Festus." Hassan said, handing Shaun two bags.

"Wow. Really? Cool man, thanks." Shaun said.

"Hey Hassan. Let me get...." I said, but I stop mid-sentence, as I watch Hassan quick limp across the street to me.

Whispering in his deep baritone scratchy voice, Hassan said,

"I know what you are."

"Know what?"

Hassan stands there facing me for a second then turns to Shaun.

"Sam Spade, take your stuff to your truck. I gotta talk to The Thin Man, alone." Hassan said, now limping back to his cart.

Shaun chews on his grapes heading to the truck. Hassan gets to his cart and starts placing blankets over the tops of his items, telling people who were coming over that he's now closed. Watching me getting more restless, Hassan reaches under his cart and pulls out a small brown satchel while he steadies his horse.

"Come with me." Hassan said, ambling away from the cart. He's tied the reins onto a stop sign pole.

Walking along with Hassan, he pulls something out of the satchel that I can't make out.

"You have become one with the wolf. I know this and I feel it. Before I came to your country, I was a 'Wab-Sekhmet', a priest, physician, a medicine man; one who possesses the skills to communicate with the spirit world and heal. Your power, rage and confusion is strong. This will stop you from becoming the beast." Hassan said, extending his closed hand.

"Old man, you must have smoked some real bad shit from the Motherland. I have no idea what you're talking about." I said, walking away from him.

Hassan grabs my right elbow, stopping my movement hard. Trying to pull away from this crazy fuck is tougher than expected, he's got a very strong grip for an old guy.

"Hassan, for real, all this shit you're saying is trippin' me out, got no time for this dumbness, if you don't let me go I'll…..!"

"You'll what? Destroy me as the beast!"

"Beast? Man, you ARE crazy!" I yell, finally breaking free of his grasp.

"You're not listening to me. Take this!" Hassan shouts, shoving a leather necklace connected to an amulet into my hand.

"What the hell is this old man?"

"It's Wepwawet, the Egyptian Wolf God. He is the opener of the way. The way you should be. Human. This will prevent….."

"Prevent what? All this is bullshit. I don't need your crazy witchcraft shit or damned stale ass fruit!" I yell, throwing the necklace back at Hassan who misses catching it.

Picking it up off the ground, anger tightens Hassan already stern face. He chants something in an African dialect, limps back to untie his horse from the pole and fast limps away. I throw my hands up in disgust walking back to the truck. Shaun's sitting in the driver's side eating his grapes shakes his head.

"What was all that about?" Shaun asks.

"Nothing. He just tried to get me to buy some shit I didn't want and he wouldn't take 'no' for an answer. Can we go now?"

"Sure dude."

7 CLUB 898

Another eventful episode. These crazy unnatural things are coming way too damned often for me. What the hell did Hassan mean by 'I know what you are', 'becoming the beast' and 'this will prevent.'? Prevent what?

This shit, Shaun calling me a werewolf, Hassan trying to give me an Egyptian Wolf God's necklace to prevent God knows what, is too much. Way too much shit to add onto the other shit I gotta think about. Fuck it. I'm going to get some rest, go to Club 898 and forget any of this happened. But I can't!

"Shaun. What was up with that 'werewolf' comment you made earlier?"

"Please don't worry about it dude, just let it go, plus I don't want to get roughed up again."

"I promise. I won't freak out on you again. Seriously." I said, extending my hand for handshake.

Shaun looks at my hand, then my face, bursting into laughter, while shaking my hand.

"Ok dude, plain logic. If you get bitten by a werewolf, like I said earlier, that person will become a werewolf, just like in the movies or books." Shaun said.

"Just like the movies and books?"

"Yeah dude, just like the movies and books."

"So you're basing your idea on a fucking movie or book you read last weekend?" I said, laughing.

"Laugh now motherfucker. When your ass grows fangs, claws and other shit, don't say shit to me!" Shaun yells.

"Hmph. I better watch out for the next full moon then huh? " I said, sarcastically.

"That's a myth asshole. I told you earlier. A werewolf can change anytime, and not of its own will. Other shit can trigger it. " Shaun said.

49

I stopped laughing.

"Shaun, how come you know so much about this shit?" I ask, waving my arms over his head mocking his supposed aura.

He ignores me.

"Shaun, come on, you and I know all this shit is way pretty far-fetched for me to believe and take seriously." I said, looking at my palm that's no longer burned.

"No problem, forget I said anything." Shaun said.

"Do we have to buy silver bullets now?" I ask.

Shaun grins sneakily driving into my parking lot. I look at what he's grinning about. It's April's car. His ass doesn't know I'm looking forward to seeing her, even though I know an argument will ensue. I truly need her reality to ground me.

"Dude. By the way, silver bullets only hurt a werewolf. When it's in human form, anything made out of Silver, burns them, but they heal fast. I think Silver mixed with Mercury can kill them though, but while in werewolf form." Shaun said.

"Yeah, ok. Whatever. Silver burns. I'll keep that in mind." I said, glancing down at my right hand.

"Good luck." Shaun said, pointing to my apartment window where we both see April looking down at us.

I turn back to Shaun as I get out of the truck easily.

"Good luck to you too brother." I said, watching Sara walking fast towards his truck.

Shaun seeing her in the reflection of April's car back window; puts the truck in reverse and speeds off, barely missing running me over. Sara's cussing is heard through the squealing tires of his get away.

I'm safe from Sara. I've already made it to my building and up one level of steps without her coming after me. Crazily, Andrew flings open his apartment door.

"Cocamoe, you're going to have to talk to your people about the crap they bring into this community."

"Hi Andrew. Bye Andrew." I said, walking past him to get to the next level of steps.

"This shit ain't funny!" Andrew shouts.

I feel my face twist in anger.

"I said BYE Andrew!" I growl.

Startled, Andrew withdraws, slams his door, engaging his many locks. I hear his heart beating hastily through his door as I smell his blood warming beneath his skin. I grip his doorknob firmly when I hear April.

"Cocamoe, what are you doing down there?"

"Just talking to Andrew." I said, turning away from his apartment door, feeling excited and thrilled by this sensation I just had.

Quickly, a new sensation replaces Andrew's bubbling blood smell. April. Her subtle lavender perfume, mixing with the scent of her lust to see me, has me quickened my pace toward her. Her scowl, greets me first, followed with her hard passionate hug and matching kiss. I lift her, pulling her closer to my body, moaning heavily as I slam the door closed. Violently and quickly, I turn her around, thrusting my left hand under her shirt, tearing feverishly at her breast. My other hand rips the buttons off her pants, pulling them down. April tries to say something, but instead, digs her nails into the back of my head as she feels me enter her. Our passion overcomes us as we fall to the ground, disjoining my leg.

"We can't be doing this right now. I'm still mad at you." she moans, trying to pull away.

I pull her closer, our feral grunts get louder and louder, then she falls limp in my arms. I release her and motion for us to go into the bathroom. We struggle to get there, removing my prosthetic eases mine.

Pulling myself up onto the shower chair, I glimpse at the clock on the soap caddy, 5:37 p.m.. My passion, right now, is still full of fever. With little restraint, I guide April onto my lap for another round. Ding!

When done, we dry each other off. With a lot less struggle, we head to my bedroom, for a little bit of shut-eye. I'm crawling to my bedroom, ass out, like I normally do after a shower. April's, seen it many times before.

"Hey baby, what's this on your stump?"

"What?"

"That mark."

"Mark? Where?"

I turn over, sitting on my ass, trying to look under my right stump. There is something there. A faint circle, with what looks like a star in the middle. I really can't make it out because of its location. April, however, was determined to get a much closer look.

"Awww baby it's nothing. Probably came from me falling the other night." I said.

Her closer look stops when I reach out to pull her on top of me.

"MMMM....Cocamoe we're taking a nap, that's it. When we wake up you can explain that horrible clean up job in the bedroom that I was not going to finish."

"Oh, that. I tried to clean that up real good but got tired. I left the window open the other night and a raccoon got in through the unscreened window into the room and bed with me. It freaked me out then my knife went into action."

"Raccoon?"

"Yup, big nasty ass raccoon. At least the smell is gone. Come on, let's get some rest baby."

I kiss April and set the alarm. She's still looking at me, and around the room strangely, then calmly cozies up under me beneath the fresh new covers shed changed, upon arrival.

We're in bed, all cuddled up, my mind free of any thought, but I can't sleep. Time passes, and I feel April moving around under the covers, like she's ready for me again. Wishful thinking on my part.

"Are we still going to Club 898 tonight baby?" she asked.

My clock on the nightstand reads 8:24 p.m., a minute before it's set to go off.

"I guess so. If you can get up." I said, kissing her nose as I reach over disabling the alarm before it does go off.

"Well, we're already clean. More than I can say for that pile of sheets in the corner" She said, smiling, removing the covers from her naked body.

I follow and start getting dressed. Her phone buzzes. She looks, but doesn't answer.

"Who's that?" I asked.

"Sara. Not in the mood for her right now."

I nod my head and continue dressing.

"Let's go slowpoke." April chides, now already dressed.

How did she beat me? Oh, I see. Long black wrap around skirt, no stockings, black leather boots, one of my white button down shirts, no bra and one of my sport jackets.

"I'll be ready woman; I'm putting on real clothes." I said, grabbing her from behind.

"Later, wild man. Later."

"Fine. Let's go then. I'm dressed." I said, somewhat miffed, brushing a thick strand of hair off my powder blue button down shirt and my khaki pants.

I walk to the front of my apartment, opening the front door for April.

"No jacket?" April asked.

"Nope. I'll be warm. That's what you're for." I said, tapping her on her ass.

We head down the stairs. On our way to the truck we come across Carlito.

"Hola, senorita, como esta? Yeah you too hombre." Carlito said, eyeing April.

"We're doing fine, thank you." I said, opening the passenger truck door for April to get in.

"Stop being mean. Hola Carlito."

Carlito smiles and walks on by. I look at him then glare at April as she scoots her ass into my truck, slightly holding the split in her dress closed. I close the door and walk to the front of the truck, stop for a second to look into the sky, looking for a full moon.

Chuckling with raised eyebrows, I continue on to the drivers side, thinking of that crazy shit Shaun said earlier. Guess it has me a bit rattled.

"What you looking for, UFO's or something?" April asks.

"Yeah. Something like that." I said, getting into the truck.

She turns on the radio, finds a cut that has her grooving in her seat and is like that the whole ride to the club. I remain quiet, admiring her movements which kept thoughts of my past weirdness at bay.

"Aren't you tired?" I ask, nearing Club 898, looking for a spot to park.

"No baby. Just getting started."

"Come on woman. I saw Shaun standing by the club entrance." I said, parking the truck a block up from the club. I disembarked and headed for the passenger side to open the door, hoping for a humdrum night.

We see Shaun outside the club, talking to a few people. As we get closer, I slow down my walk, to check out April. Her outfit is slutty and classy. Well, as classy as any slut can be. That wrap-around dress accents her lower body very nicely. She's wearing her hair wild, unkempt, but in a stylish manner. Her intention is to dance, sweat and have a good time. Our sexual cat and mouse game is turning me on, again.

"'Bout damn time! It's 10:15!" Shaun shouts.

"We're here, be thankful, dammit!" I shout back.

April embraces Shaun long, making his eyes glow.

"Ok, that's enough of that shit." I said, playfully separating the two.

"Don't worry, I have a date dude." Shaun said, releasing April.

"I know. Kari. Where is she?" I ask.

Shaun looks at me, surprised.

"She's inside. How'd you know she's here?"

"Lucky guess. Let's get inside." I said, I couldn't tell him that I smell her sex all over him.

"Cool beans. I haven't seen Kari in a while." April said, holding both our hands like a little kid as we enter the club.

We make a momentary stop at the ticket booth so I can pay mine and April's cover. The three of us walk through the glass enclosed foyer of Club 898, when April breaks free of our grip. She's running to Kari standing by the front bar. When they embrace, Kari slightly lifts April off the ground, exposing her leg through the split. Then Kari kisses her wildly on the lips. Interesting. Shaun is eyeing the female bartender with the tight fitting t-shirt at the front bar. Typical.

Club 898's crowd size is moderate, right now. I'm still watching April and Kari's giddy playful gestures towards one another; touching, admiring each others outfits and holding hands. Kari's mini skirt with tattered stockings and ankle boots were much better than that drab waitress outfit I normally see her in. Those boots define her calf muscles well and her t-shirt was just as tight as the bartenders, but perkier. Thoughts of me, her and

April get interrupted by Shaun.

"Dude! What you drinking?" Shaun shouts.

I wave him off. My attention is on four open seats at a table against the wall. I get closer to April and Kari, wrap my arms around their waists and escort them that way. People check us out, some in jealous anger, others full of longing.

Minutes after we sit, here comes Shaun to the table. He has a beer bottle in his mouth that he's holding in place with his teeth because both hands are holding two Apple Martinis for the ladies. April and Kari kiss him on his cheek, while he still has the beer bottle in his mouth. He's blushing..

After an hour or so, Club 898 is jammed packed. The four of us dance to the House music, entrancing us all into wild rhythmic impromptu moves. In between dancing we talk; greet those we know and dance some more, all having a great ass time.

I'm getting thirsty.

"I'll be back; I'm going to the bar to get some water. Y'all want anything?" I shout.

"Water!" they all yell.

I give the thumbs up and head to the bar in the rear. My trip there has me taking in the sights, smells and sounds when out of nowhere the sights, smells and sounds take me in. Laughter, talking, screaming, House music, body parts jiggling, perfumes, oils, sex, body odor and digested food have me stumbling, disoriented falling against the moving crowd. Dazed, I try to regain my balance and bearings. I can hear people saying things like;

"He's too effed-up to be going to some damned bar."

"I hope his ass ain't driving."

I try to pinpoint these voices, but it's too much, making me more confused and disoriented. I do make it to the rear bar, bumping hard into a guy standing there.

"Yo. Watch it my man!" he yells.

"My bad sir, I'm sorry!"

"Damn right it's your bad, mother....Hey, Cocamoe. Joe Cocamoe. Ain't this a bitch!" The guy I bumped into shouts.

I take a few steps back, closing my eyes trying to get a hold of myself. When I open them and focus, I see it's Sammy, Sammy Forbes. He was brought in by me four or five years ago, one of my first clients. I don't know if it was me looking at Sammy's ugly mug or smelling his bad breath but the ratchet sounds and smells strangling me have gone back to normal.

"Hey, Sammy. I heard you were out. Why'd you come back to Baltimore? Thought Memphis was more you!" I yell, trying to keep my guard and myself upright.

"You're still Mr. Funny-ass. Ain't he, Cliff!" Sammy yells, placing his huge hand on my shoulder.

The guy next to Sammy must be Cliff, he's someone I've never seen before. I'd definitely remember a motherfucker with a thick bulging ear to ear length welt under his chin. He just squints at me then turns his back and continues drinking.

"Yo. Cocamoe. Let me get your drink."

"That's okay. I got it. Thanks though." I shout, smiling at Sammy but keeping an eye on Cliff.

"What! I ain't good enough for you or something?"

"Naw, nothing like that at all, I'm just getting water anyway!"

"Water! What a coincidence, that's what me and Cliff is drinking. Hey bartender, 3 more waters over here!" Sammy screams.

Before I could refuse again, the bartender has already handed three cups of water to Cliff. Who in turn, hands the cups to Sammy.

"Here you go bounty man. No hard feelings." Sammy said, leaning in close..

I think he's tired of yelling, I wish he had continued yelling but in another direction. He raises his cup to mine in a toasting manner. I raise mine in return, tapping his cup, then reach forward and tap Cliff's.

"Sammy it was nice seeing you and your buddy, Cliff, but I gotta get back to my date!" I yell, drinking the last of my water.

This time, I'm yelling at the bartender.

"Hey! Three more cups of water, please!"

The bartender brings them over and I say my goodbyes to them both. Sammy playfully punches me in my arm. Cliff winks at me with an eerie smile brandished across his face, as I walk away. The distortion I had earlier is gone, so I'm able to ease my way back to our table with no problem.

"What took you so long baby!?" April shouts.

"Saw a very old friend!" I shout back, pointing towards the rear bar at Sammy and Cliff.

"Who are they?" she asks, leaning closer to me.

"The big guy is Sammy an old runner, one of my first bounties. The other guy I don't know, just met him." I shout.

"Oh."

Where's Shaun?" I shout, moving closer to Kari.

"He went outside. Got a phone call, said it was important. It better be!" Kari shouts.

Across the street from Club 898, Shaun is talking to his cousin, Detective Norris.

"I was trying to tell you earlier but you blew me off. The blood at the murder scene in Seawell State Park the other day matches the blood taken from where your Bounty Hunter partner was found naked that same day." Detective Norris said.

"Blood? Naked? Cocamoe? What the hell are you talking about?"

"I see, your partner didn't tell you about his mishap the other night. Well, he was found naked in the Seawell State Park by a jogger who called Northwest District requesting me to come to the scene. I was already in the park investigating a brutal murder there. I eventually made it to where your partner was and he told me about him getting robbed, and stripped naked in the park. Oh, they took his leg too. Your partner doesn't remember a thing about it, so he says." Detective Norris said.

"I....I see. That's why that bastard drove to the park earlier today." Shaun mumbles.

"What was that?" Detective Norris asked.

"Nothing. I'll talk to you later. Thanks for telling me cuz."

"Late..." the phone disconnected.

Shaun races back into the club, fighting his way through the crowd of people still trying to get in. Once inside, he cuts through a swarm of people on the dance floor, to get to Kari and April.

"Baby, what's wrong? You okay?" April asks me, as I suddenly double over holding my stomach.

I'm queasy and short of breath. Taking a sip of Shaun's water seems to make it worse.

"Tiger(not animal?), what's going on?" Kari asks.

"Nothing ladies. Just gotta hit the men's room. Be right back." I said.

"You need an escort!" April shouts.

"NO! I'll be okay." I yell, walking briskly towards the bathroom.

Wrangling my way through the fluid chaos of the House music crowd, my vision gets slightly blurred and my head pounds. For a quick second, I thought I saw Shaun on the other side of the dance floor.

I make it to the bathroom door. Sweat is springing out of me and I'm hacking repeatedly. I pull hard on the door handle to get into the small ass bathroom; two stalls, two sinks and one urinal. Three guys inside instantly move out of my way as I bolt to an open stall. I'm thinking that asshole Sammy has poisoned me.

"You alright man?" A voice asked.

"Yeah." I gurgle, placing my head above the toilet, waiting to vomit.

It's a false alarm. Something else is happening. My body's hot, very hot. My right leg throbs rapidly, causing my stump to squeeze hard against my prosthetic socket. Gotta get this leg off, it hurts and stings like a bitch. I quickly pull down my khakis to undo my prosthetic.

"AWWW FUCK!" Cocamoe, screams out.

"You sure you're okay man?" A nervous voice squelches out.

Unnervingly, the toilet stall door and the surrounding structures splinter, exploding laminated wood throughout the bathroom. The repugnant werewolf unveiled.

It grabs the closest human, unhinging the poor souls intestines onto the grimy, piss stained floor. As that body hammers to the floor, the other two men fight each other to get the hell out of the door. The werewolf bites the back of the neck of one of the men, sending the head careening into the mirror, splattering into the sink. The headless body falls hard into the bathroom door forcing it open. It's body crashes into the hallway, horrifying the couple fucking in the dark corner against the wall. Their sexcapade entanglement makes them witnesses to the fate of the last man in the bathroom. He's being gutted ferociously from behind. Blood, intestines and other organs slam onto the bathroom floor, mixing with the other man's innards. The woman screaming wildly, pushes hard against her lover, disengaging enough to run away from the wretchedness to the dance floor. Her lover, not so fortunate. He tries running under the elongated arms of the beast but is grabbed and raised above the werewolf's head. It snaps the man's body in half, engulfing his dislodged bowels into its waiting mouth.

There's massive disorder in Club 898. People running to get out, many not knowing what the hell they're running from, just running. The werewolf, entrenched and dripping of human bowels, leaps from the bathroom area onto the rear bar, where Sammy and Cliff still are, stuck by the crush of people. Cliff tries desperately to unholster the gun he snuck into the club, but it's no use; the werewolf places its arms on both sides of the men and squeezes them together until their bodies explode all over the werewolf, the terror stricken crowd, and the bar. The werewolf reaches down, gobbling, chomping and slurping the remains of the two.

Kari, hyperventilating as she too tries to run, falls into her chair hard. With head whirling, she fades in and out of consciousness. April, eyes and mouth agape, witnesses the squirting blood, the floundering of unattached body parts, and the desecrated souls cohesive, into a dance only hell can choreograph. Shaun, too, is in disbelief at what he's viewing. His protective instinct kicks in. He reaches down, pulling Kari up, then grabbing April. The werewolf's carnage is getting closer.

"We've got to go! NOW!" Shaun screams.

He gets them both out of a side emergency door near where they were sitting and leads them to his truck.

"Where's Cocamoe?" Shaun yells, looking behind him at people trying to get out.

"Don't know. He went to the bathroom then all hell broke loose!" April screams.

"What is that thing!?" Kari screams, hysterically, trying to catch her breath.

"I don't know! I don't know!" April yells.

Shaun opens his truck passenger door, quickly placing the two ladies inside. He unlocks a compartment behind the passenger seat and pulls out his gun and two clips. He inserts one into the gun, the other clip he puts in his pocket.

"April. Here are the keys. Go to Central City Police District. It's not far. Go there and stay. I'll go find Cocamoe. Everything's gonna be fine. Drive! Go. Go now!" Shaun shouts, looking intently at Kari as they pull off.

Shaun runs to the front entrance of Club 898. Escaping party goers are jumping over the injured and the dead. The once pristine foyer is fragmented into broken wooden frames. Traumatized glass is adorned with tattered clothing and blood. Lights still rotate and blink, syncing with House music blaring from the 24" speakers on the walls and ceiling. The echo of the voice in the song makes the carnage and destruction surreal. Shaun jumps from his image in the mirrors plastered throughout the club. His nervousness dwindles slightly when he decides to use them to his advantage, informing him where that thing may be.

He starts thinking that whatever that thing is, it may be his partner, Cocamoe. He prays it isn't. Too much weird shit has happened between the two in the past few days. Those occurrences flash through Shaun's mind; their violent confrontations, Cocamoe's new taste for raw meat and that craziness in Lloyd's with the silver fork. Silver burns werewolves in human form.

Shaun wants to call out Cocamoe's name. He may be trapped somewhere hurt, needing his help. This will also prove himself wrong about the werewolf thing, but calling out will definitely bring unwanted attention. Shaun's attention is throttled when he hears something drop in the rear of the club. Quickly, he positions himself and his gun in the direction of the sound, crouching behind an upturned table, waiting. Several minutes pass and nothing happens. Shaun gets up to walk to the rear of the club when he hears a new sound; one not in sync with the blaring music. Crunching, crackling, rapid chewing and muffled growls. This unnatural sound is coming from behind the bar, then it stops. He's five feet away from the end of the rear bar using the bottles of liquor behind the bar to see if there is a reflection of the werewolf. Nothing. No movement at all.

Now in a walking crouched position, Shaun passes the rear bar, coming across the remains of one, or more bodies. Flinching a little, he notices a shot glass with an unused shot of something on top of the bar. Picking up the shot glass sniffing the tequila, Shaun wolfs it down, forcing his eyes closed, briefly. They should've stayed closed.

The ghastly wholeness of the creature is presented to Shaun. Seven to eight feet in height. Massive muscular shoulders, long powerful fury arms, dark black fur with sprinkles of gray. Clumps of dark scarlet blood and human remains are smeared on the werewolf's face, chest and paw extensions. Its eyes large and placid, almost hypnotic. It's the monster's elongated snout bearing blood debased razor sharp teeth that paralyze Shaun with fear.

The werewolf's fetid hell smell rapidly encloses Shaun's soul as it deliberately comes even closer. Somehow, this snaps Shaun out of his statue state. Looking down, he sees the position of where his gun is aimed at the creature's abdomen. The werewolf's saliva, mixed with its victims blood and meat, drips onto Shaun's chest. That's when he fires the gun. It howls loudly, staggering away from Shaun. The gun's loaded with silver bullets, and an extra kick. Mercury.

Shaun fires again, hitting the werewolf in its left leg, making it flinch and yelp. It jumps at Shaun but he ducks having the creature fly over his head. The werewolf rapidly re-positions itself for another jump when more shots are fired into its body. Howling louder, smoke billows from its wounds.

Turning away from Shaun, the werewolf leaps to the front of the club, disappearing. Shaun, feeling cocky and confident, senses the added touch of mercury may hurt the werewolf more than expected. However, that feeling is overtaken by the fact that this thing is more than likely his best friend, his partner, his brother, Joseph Cocamoe. With hesitation and some remorse, Shaun loads the other mercury laced silver clip into his gun.

Walking to the front of Club 898, near the front bar, Shaun tries to stay focused. Hell, earlier that night he was eyeing the bartender with the tight t-shirt. Presently, he is hunting a damned werewolf which he sees in the large mirror behind the bar.

"Got your ass now. Sorry brother." Shaun whispers, raising his gun while stepping on a chair to be as quiet as possible, to get on top of the bar itself.

Shaun's watching the reflection of the werewolf; it looks hurt, curled in a large ball on the floor. With great caution and still on top of the bar, Shaun inches to the area where it lays. In the back of Shaun's mind, he wonders why it hasn't heard him.

Within a flash, the werewolf vaults into the bar itself, disintegrating the area where Shaun once stood. He flies into the already fallen chairs and tables, separating him from his gun. Frenzied, Shaun feels around the club's floor for the gun. Flashing spinning lights make it more difficult to get any perception of distance. In a moment of focus, Shaun sees the gun between himself and the werewolf, which is now on all fours, pacing. Each flash of the spinning lights reveal a different bodily contortion of damnation by the werewolf. Its pain and the processing of it is new.

Unexpectedly, Shaun screams out

"Cocamoe, Joe Cocamoe! Is that you?! It's me. Your partner. Your brother. Shaun!"

The werewolf, doesn't stop pacing. It threads slowly over to the gun sniffing. Smelling the mercury, it tosses the gun to the rear of the club.

Rising onto its hind legs, it displays the bullet wounds, as if to say 'you can't kill me'. Foolishly, Shaun runs, incensing the werewolf. A fast deep cutting swipe of its paw spills Shaun innards to the floor.. Rhythmic beats and droning from the cadre of speakers, are overwhelmed by the werewolf's howl as it thrusts deeper into Shaun.

Kari and April, safe inside Central City District, the main police headquarters in downtown Baltimore, watch officers responding to the hell happening at Club 898. They are told to have a seat and the duty officer will get to them in a minute. Not one officer is stopping. They're rushing to get to the site, yelling at one another in all the excitement;

"What weapons do we need for this shit!?" one officer shouts.

"Take it all, we're now hunting huge fucking animals in nightclubs!" another officer excitedly shouts.

Several nervous looking officers, fumbling with their utility belts, rifles, gas masks and riot shields run pass Kari and April.

"You won't need these!" a senior officer yells, knocking the gas mask and shield from their hands.

All officers will be facing an unprecedented horror.

"You know this is bullshit!" April yells.

"No one is going to help us. We should go back to the club and look for our men." Kari said gravely, clutching April's hand, pulling her to the door. April, knowing better, grabs Kari and walks her away from the throngs of madness, smelling her own disbelief.

Once inside Shaun's truck, April floors it North up an empty Guilford Avenue, a one way street southbound. Her route beats the Central City District Officers to the chaos and hell that hasn't left.

8 CARNAGE

Inside Club 898, bodies, dead and alive, are everywhere. Central City District Patrol Officers and EMT personnel administer to the petrified club goers. Someone turns off the music but not the spinning lights. Detective Norris, way out of his jurisdiction, is here searching for his cousin Shaun.

Norris steps over trampled crushed bodies, slathers of blood, shredded clothes, glass and body parts. Dreading what he'll find inside, he continues on, silently repeating,

"I've seen shit like this before, I can handle this."

Nevertheless, no human should see what he's seeing now.

Norris shows his credentials to one of the patrol officers to fully enter the club.

"Detective, we've found something!" a patrol officer shouts.

Detective Norris steps around a large overturned chair, slipping on something on the floor. Catching his balance, he looks at what tripped him up. A mangled forearm ripped from the elbow. Pulling a small flashlight from his inside coat pocket, Norris leans closer to get a better view of the blood covered watch. This watch is a familiar one.

"Shit!" Norris shouts, fumbling with the flashlight.

It's Shaun. He recognizes the watch as the one Norris gave him when he received his Bounty Hunter's license.

"Hey. I want this bagged. Now!" Detective Norris yells, trying to remain composed.

"Yes sir! Was this photo'd already, gentlemen?" a distant voice rings out.

"I'm doing it now!" a Crime Scene member screams out.

The patrol officer, who initially shouted that they found something, waits there patiently for Detective Norris.

"Let's go." Norris bellows, as he follows the patrol officer into the rear bathroom.

They're walking to the bathroom, through an erector set of body parts, blood and organs, spread across the floor and bar counter.

"Watch your step, Sir." the patrol officer said, taking a wide step over the lower half of a person's torso in the front half of the hallway.

Norris looks down, side-stepping it slowly, shines his flashlight on the torso, hoping it isn't part of Shaun too. There's some relief, as it doesn't look like Shaun; however, there are more mangled bodies in the bathroom.

"Over here sir." the patrol officer said, motioning for Detective Norris to come to what used to be the furthest bathroom stall.

"This is what we found near this stall."

Detective Norris stands there staring at what's presented. A prosthetic leg and ripped clothing.

"What do you make of that, Sir?" the patrol officer asks.

"Not sure, yet. Another item to photo and bag, guys!" Norris shouts, looking at the demolished toilet stall.

"Look at what the dog dug up!" a voice chimes out.

Detective Norris exhales, knowing to whom the voice belongs. Detective Laboo from Central City Police District, looking like a Hollywood movie detective. His thousand dollar suit, shoes that cost a little more, and tie that may cost more than the shoes and suit combined, seemed grossly out of context. All draped upon a home gym built body. He's clean shaven. Tight, short afro with a slightly wrinkled face, always donning sunglasses, displaying a phony "cool" look, inside a crime scene. At night. They haven't seen or spoken to one another in years and Norris vividly remembers why.

"Out of your jurisdiction, Norris. What, were you here getting your groove on?" Detective Laboo said, slightly twisting his hips.

With a straight face and maintaining professional restraint, Norris does his best to not punch Laboo.

"Shaun was here tonight. He's dead." Norris said, eyeing the severed head in the sink.

"Shaun? Your little cousin Shaun? Mmmm...real sorry to hear that." Detective Laboo said.

Both men stand there silent for a brief moment then are interrupted by the sound of an officer vomiting in the toilet.

"Flush that officer. We don't want any forensic confusion." Laboo said, smirking, looking around the bathroom, this time without his sunglasses.

"Who could've done some shit like this? In all my 29 years on the force and 2 tours in Desert Storm, I've never seen anything like this." Detective Laboo said, stooping low to look at a body part under the sink.

"Yeah. Real bad situation. Make sure your forensics people get everything, and don't get any blood on your suit." Detective Norris said, walking out of the bathroom, as more forensic members make their way toward the bathroom.

"Don't worry about them, Norris, or my gear. Hey hold up, I've got some questions for you." Detective Laboo said, chasing behind Detective Norris, avoiding the forensics team, too.

"What could you possibly have to ask me!"

"Look, I'm really sorry about Shaun and all, but do you know if he was here on business, or pleasure. You know how those bounty guys are. Speaking of bounty guys, where's his partner, the main guy, Cocamoe?"

Just then, one of the forensic members walks past the two detectives with several clear bags of evidence. One of the clear bags has the prosthetic leg in it and tattered clothing. Laboo stops him to look at the bag.

"Don't that beat all. A fake leg. Someone was in a real hurry to leave that behind."

"Yeah." Detective Norris said, turning away from Detective Laboo.

Before Detective Laboo could follow up on his previous question about 'where is Cocamoe', another thought pops into his head, 'Cocamoe wears a fake leg'.

An EMT yells, "Detectives, we've got a guy back here in the alley!"

The two detectives rush to the rear door into the poorly lit alley. Norris silently remarks how clean the alley is, albeit two overturned trash cans lay next to a body two EMT's were working on. Norris peers at the man's face between the two medics.

"Cocamoe?" Norris said.

Detective Laboo, now without his sunglasses, adjusts his eyes to the light from the EMT's ambulance.

"Why the hell is he naked and what's the deal with his leg? Oh shit, yeah that leg in the...." Detective Laboo said, but he's cut off by one of the medics.

"This man is alive but not doing well, we have to transport him to the hospital immediately, Sirs."

"Wait, I've got some questions for Mr. Cocamoe!" Detective Norris yells.

"My jurisdiction, Norris. I'll be asking the damned questions!"

The EMT ignores both detectives, and positions the gurney next to Cocamoe.

"Sirs, we've gotta move this Cocamoe fellow now. All questions can be asked at the hospital!"

During the confrontation between the two detectives and the EMT's, April and Kari are at the entrance of the alley, being held back by several officers, when April hears Cocamoe's name.

"Cocamoe! Joe! Joe!" she yells, trying to get pass the officers.

Then she pulls out her nurse badge which she always has for those 'just in case' moments. One of the officers looking at her badge lets her through and she squeezes out of the crowd, taking hold of Kari, pulling her through too. Both detectives seeing two women rushing down the alley quickly confront them.

"Hey! Who the hell let y'all down here? You two shouldn't be here!" Detective Laboo shouts.

"I'm trying to get to Cocamoe, I'm his girlfriend and a nurse. Is he OK?" April said.

"He's fine, he's fine. They're taking him to the hospital, April." Detective Norris said, trying to escort them back to the crowd at the front of the alley.

"You know these two ladies?" detective Laboo asked.

"Yeah. Be cool, Laboo."

"Where's Shaun?" Kari asks, looking behind the detectives at the police, EMT's, crime lab team and a few victims scattered about.

Norris doesn't answer.

"Where the hell is Shaun?" Kari yells.

"Kari, ….Shaun's dead."

"What….."

April takes hold of Kari's arm to steady her rapidly decreasing equilibrium.

"I'm so sorry Kari." Detective Norris said, placing his hand on her shoulder.

"Me too ma'am, real sorry." Detective Laboo said, watching the medics load Cocamoe into the ambulance.

Kari pulls away from them, trying to get into the club. April, instinctively jumps in front, embracing her tightly. She, herself, not truly believing what she just heard.

Gently, but with some force, April walks the distraught Kari away from the two detectives back to the front of the alley and crowd. Halfway through the throngs of people she whispers to Kari,

"I am sooo sorry about Shaun. I'm here for you in any possible way. Honey, listen to me though, we've got to find out for ourselves what's going on. Are you going to be able to handle this Kari, 'cause I'm really going to need you?"

Kari shakes nods her head, pushing away tears.

"They're gonna take Cocamoe to Trinity hospital. It's one mile away, that's where we're going too." April said, still holding onto Kari.

They watch the two detectives run to their respective cars to follow the ambulance. Seeing this, April and Kari fight through the onslaught of police, EMT's and onlookers to get to Shaun's truck, to follow, as well. Once inside the truck, April sits there, stoic and cold. Looking straight ahead collecting herself before she eventually starts the truck's engine, pulling off.

"April."

"Yes."

"What the hell just happened? What was that thing in the club? What….. was it? It killed my Shaun, it killed my Shaun…" Kari said, softly.

9 HOSPITAL

April reaches out, placing her right hand on Kari's shoulder as the name Trinity appears a few feet in front of the tattered 'EMERGENCY' sign on the outer wall of the hospital. She swings the truck into the parking lot and parks in some doctor's assigned spot.

"Kari sweetheart, you want to stay here in the truck, or come with me?"

"I'm coming with you. That thing may still be out here!" Kari nervously said.

The two ladies rush into the emergency room entrance when they are stopped by Detective Norris.

"Whoa, hold up ladies, slow ya roll. You two should be home or something" Norris said.

"Please get out of our way, Norris!" April yells.

"Ladies he's sedated so you must wait, just like us." Detective Laboo blurts out.

Both ladies ease their willingness to get past the two detectives.

"What room did they take him to?" April asks.

"724." Detective Laboo said.

April tries again to slip around Norris when he takes hold of her arm.

"He's sedated dammit!" Detective Norris, shouts in a hushed tone.

Lucy, a Trinity ER nurse, hearing the conversation, recognizes April.

"April. Hi sweetheart. I heard the conversation about your friend who was brought here. I'll make arrangements for you to stay with him in his room. You, detective, will have to wait." Lucy said.

April, relieved that Lucy appears, turns to a pissed off Norris.

"Norris, can you take Kari home please, she's afraid?"

Detective Norris, on the verge of cursing April out, calms down, changing his tone.

"Sure, I'll take her home and assign a unit to watch her house."
April smiles, hugging detective Norris.

"Can you answer one question April before I leave? Please?" Detective Norris asks.

Lucy cuts a cold eye at Norris.

"Yeah, ok, one." April said.

"What happened at the club?" Norris asks, watching Detective Laboo gawk at the nurses walking by.

"We get in club, Shaun gets us some drinks, we grab a table, do some dancing, then Cocamoe goes to get us water. He comes back, says he ran into a guy he apprehended long time ago, then he said he felt a little sick. Cocamoe goes to bathroom, Shaun was outside taking your call. He came back in, and all hell broke loose. That thing attacking all those people. Those poor unsuspecting people."

"Thing? What was this thing?"

"I don't know? Big ass dog, escaped zoo animal, mutant wolf. Whatever it was, it was big as shit, nasty and horrifying."

"So you saw it real well?"

"Too well."

"So it looked like a big ass dog, mutant wolf or something." Norris repeats, while writing down what's said.

"That's when Shaun got me and Kari out of the club, then he went back in to get Cocamoe." April said, breaking down, crying.

"Okay detective, that's enough." Lucy said.

Detective Laboo, now noticing something isn't right, fast approaches Norris. Ignoring the nurse he was talking to.

"Norris, what are you doing? Are you questioning my witness?"

"No Laboo. Your jurisdiction, remember?" Norris said.

April, calming herself, gets Kari to go along with Norris. Kari complying, walks with Norris, guiding her to the ER exit, when she yanks away, shouting,

"It was a damned werewolf people! A God-damned werewolf! It's going to kill us all! All of us!"

Patients, staff and those in the waiting room look up. Most of them, more than likely heard or saw what happened at Club 898 on the television, radio or cell phone.

Immediately Detective Norris takes hold of Kari, covering her mouth, and escorts her out of ER.

"Werewolf? Maybe she should stay here too and be sedated?" Lucy said.

Half-smiling, April looks out the large ER windows, watching Norris and a seemingly calmer Kari get into his car. Walking closer to the ER windows, April looks up into the dark moonless sky. Lucy stops, looking upwards too.

"What we looking for honey?"

"A miracle." April whispers.

"Let's get you to that room hon. Tonight's going to be very busy." Lucy said, as more ambulances roll into the ER parking lot.

"I bet."

"I'd better call upstairs to tell them know you'll be staying in 724 tonight." Lucy said, pulling the hospital cell phone from her pocket.

"Seventh floor." Carol, a seventh floor nurse said.

"Hi Carol, this is Lucy in ER. Can you get room 724 setup for a guest please? Yeah. I'm bringing her up now. Thanks."

"It's all set." Lucy said.

Standing in front of the Staff Only elevator, Lucy smiles at April, reassuring her everything's going to be ok. The elevator arrives and Lucy punches in the security code so they can enter. April follows her in and leans against the rear wall, mentally and physically worn out.

"I've never seen anything like that, ever. It was the stuff you see in the movies or some way too creative Indie film student's project. But this shit was real life." April said, solemnly.

"Honey, don't worry too much about what happened and what you saw. There has to be a logical and reasonable explanation for it all. You're safe now." Lucy said.

"You weren't there. No one is safe."

The elevator door opens. Several hospital employees moving around the floor pay little attention to who's getting off.

"This way sweetie." Lucy said, guiding April to the right.

At the room, Lucy gently pushes open 724's door. Dim emerald and amber lights from the blood pressure and IV machines, cast a sinister shadow on Cocamoe, lying peacefully asleep with his back to them. Also in the room with him is a wide hospital visitor chair near the entrance and a folded out cot. The cot, neatly made up with an extra blanket, a pillow and a box of toiletries, is near the window. April, both worried, but joyful, walks to Cocamoe's bed to plant a kiss on him. All at once, Cocamoe springs up. Pulling April closer, he rips through her neck with God forsaken jagged sharp teeth, painting a bloody horrific mural onto the hospital walls. His face, is that of the thing from the club.

April falls back hard and fast into Lucy's arms.

"My God hon. He just yawned, that's all. He just yawned. Are you ok? You really need to calm yourself. You sure you want to stay here tonight?" Lucy said, in a hushed tone holding April upright. "Yes. I'm okay, I'm fine. I don't know what came over me or where that even came from. I'll be fine, really. Thanks." April said, reaching for the wide visitor chair to sit.

"Are you sure?" Lucy said, feeling behind April's ears, checking her pulse.

"I'm okay, really. I guess that was a delayed reaction to all the shit I went through today."

"Well you're not hot, no fever, pulse is racing but you did just kinda freak out. Do I have to get you a sleeping pill?"

"No. Lucy, for real, I'm okay. Really."

"Okay sweetie. I'll remind the floor duty nurse you're here and that you'll be staying. Get yourself some rest, and I'll check on you in the AM. You sure you're going to be okay?"

"Yes. I'm okay. Thank you, thank you for everything."

Lucy looks at April then glances at the sleeping Cocamoe. "He'll be out for a while. It's 2:55 a.m. now. They gave him a powerful sedative when he got here." Lucy said, looking at his chart.

"Great, then I can get some sleep too." April said, looking at the sleeping Cocamoe.

Lucy, convinced that April is calm, finally leaves the room. Cocamoe slowly turns fully onto his back, startling April, again. Her ease comes when she sees his face is his. Letting out her anxiety, she gets out of the chair to go the cot.

"Cool, chewing gum." April said, checking out the box on toiletries. Unwrapping a piece, she chews, keeping an eye on Cocamoe. She relaxes, calming down more with the gum. Succumbing to the rough night she's had, she lays her head down on the pillow, fast falling asleep.

Once again, I'm waking up in unfamiliar surroundings. Before going spastic, I smell a familiar smell. Sniffing again then slowly raising up, I see April, my baby, asleep on a cot next to me. Where the fuck are we?

Trying my best not to wake her, I carefully look around my new wake up spot. Looks like I'm either in a hospital room or a mental institution room.

I hear unfamiliar voices outside the door.

"I'm sure he's still asleep. You don't have much to worry about officer. It is 3:20 AM."

Then the door opens. I close my eyes and lay still in the bed.

"I don't want to wake her up so I'll make it quick." she whispers to herself.

She goes on to check my temperature, blood pressure and my IV. I have a hard time acting unconscious when she pulls back my eyelids, I guess she's a nurse. Then as quickly as she came in, she leaves. Reopening my eyes, I adjust them seeing April's still asleep. There are a pair of crutches leaning against the wall five feet from my bed. April ain't gonna like it, but I've gotta get outta here and do it without her.

Quietly, I place my left leg over the side of the bed, being careful of this IV in my right arm. I press the 'off' button on the IV machine, making sure it's truly off before I pull the IV out of my arm. No beeping, so out it comes.

Neither Cocamoe, nor the hospital staff, are aware that the sedatives had no effect on him at all. He was asleep because he wanted to be. After the large feeding he had as a werewolf, his long rest was warranted.

"Shit. Since I'm without a leg, I'll do just like I do at home when I don't have it on." I whisper to myself, stroking my confidence while praying the hospital bed's headboard is stable enough for my weight.

I hold tight onto the headboard and maneuver my ass to those crutches. Got them. I'll check to see if my leg is anywhere here then check for my clothes. Opening the patient closet to find it empty is not a good sign. The one drawer at the bottom of the closet is empty too. There are no clothes or prosthetic in the bathroom either. This hospital gown and crutches will have to do. Still haven't awaken April, good. My next problem is that officer outside my door. I could just kill him but I don't want a murder charge.

Cracking the door open slowly, I see him sitting in a chair, reading the sports page of the newspaper. Very clearly, I see the score of all the hoop games I missed, despite the small print. Gently, I open the door wider. Seeing the hallway empty and no one's at the nurses desk, I begin to move toward the officer. Quickly, I apply a "sleeper hold" on the unsuspecting officer, my other arm supporting my weight on these crutches helps me finish the job. Doing this was kinda clumsy. I made sure to keep shifting my weight and pull him close but not too close. One slip and he's either dead, or my ass falls and gets caught.

Checking on April, I see she's still asleep. I carefully drag the officer into my room by shifting my weight carefully, slowly and quiet. Using the wall as leverage to move, I place him softly against the wall. I still need to figure a way out of this room and hospital. Maybe the size of this officer can help. He's tall like me, but skinny as shit. The length of his uniform may work but his pants may not get over my thighs. Having no real other choice, I start delicately undressing the officer. Not worried about rousing him, more worried about waking April.

"Get the fuck outta here, these pants fit, with his keys in the pocket too. Tight, but manageable." I say to myself.

My surprise has me rush a bit. Getting his shirt on, his nameplate falls off, clinking loudly onto the floor. Must've loosed it when I gave him the sleeper move. April moves around some on her cot but she doesn't wake up. I position his shirt fully up on my shoulders and it fits me like a glove. He probably wears a size larger to compensate for the bullet proof vest. I'm all set, except a shoe. Can't leave barefoot. His all black sneaker looks about my size. It's a snug fit. I'd rather snug than loose when it comes to a shoe. I don't want that shit coming off and me busting my ass.

Dressed and ready to roll out, I saw a stairway a few feet away from my room, where I put the officer to sleep. My brain works overtime on a plan to get out.

I'll walk down one flight to avoid being seen by staff on this floor, get on elevator there, go to ground level, take officers car. By the time they realize I ain't there and the officers car is gone, I'll be home with my own clothes and extra leg. Good plan, very good plan, piece of cake.

Without hesitation, I hobble out of my room to the stairwell without anyone seeing me. Now, down these damned steps with crutches and one leg. The first four steps down are a pain in the ass. Granted, I've moved around many times at home without my leg, but very seldom do I use crutches.

Almost busting my ass down the steps, I place the crutches under my left arm, hold tight to the railing and hop down the remaining steps. That was somewhat treacherous, especially with these tight ass police pants, but I got the hang of it and regained my balance.

I get to the door of the sixth floor, and ease it open to take a look into the hallway. Clear, no one around. Placing a crutch under each underarm I make my way to the elevator, push the down button and wait.

"May I help you?"

Shit. I'm busted. I act like I don't hear the voice but it came again.

"Officer? Are you ok?."

Wow, she called me officer. Slowly turning to face the voice I get a very pleasant surprise. This young, beautiful, fair skinned woman with the cutest dimples and a military buzz cut crowning her head stands before me. I'm admiring her beauty so much I almost forgot what she said.

"Yes. I'm a patient…" I said, but she cuts me off.

"Oh, a patient. You'll need a wheelchair to go around the hospital, you know, until you get used to those crutches. Sorry about your leg." the young nurse said, probably noticing my struggle to get to the elevator. Don't know how I didn't hear or smell her with my sometimey new heightened senses.

"Oh. Yeah, guess you're right." I said.

"Wait right here."

I smile, leaning against the wall.

"Where are you headed?" the young nurse asks, coming back pushing an empty wheelchair.

"To my car. My partner parked downstairs and I want to get some items out of it. He doesn't want to see me like this so we planned it this way. I'm single so he left me some clothes, all I have in my room is my uniform and hospital gown since my surgery earlier this week, plus I can't sleep."

"No problem. I'll take you officer."

"Sure."

The young nurse locks the wheelchair and holds onto the wheelchair bars as I plop my ass down. Unlocking the wheels, she pushes me to the staff elevator. The door opens with two male orderlies exiting. They smile and greet my escort, ignoring me. Good.

She smiles back, enters her code into the keypad and we head down. I'm thinking I should pay a visit to Hassan along with the other shit I have to do. Not exactly sure where he lives but I have an idea where to find him.

"I'm Ashley."

"I'm Otis, Office Otis. Nice to meet you" I said, smiling, looking at the faded name 'Otis' on the elevator floor.

"Nice to meet you too, Officer Otis. Here we are." she said, as the elevator stops.

"Cool."

"Where is your car, oh never mind, I see it. Hold on tight, there is a bump here."

There are several nurses at the ER desk but they never look up from their computers to notice me, or Ashley. She wheels me out to the parking lot to the rear of the patrol car and I get confused. Then it clicks, I told her my stuff is in the trunk.

Fumbling with the keys, I get the trunk open. Of course there's nothing of mine there, just his typical cop shit.

"My partner must of put it in the front seat." I said, wheeling the chair myself to the driver's side door, unlocking it.

I'm having a slight problem adjusting the wheelchair to be level with the patrol car seat.

"Ashley...."

"Oh, I'm sorry." Ashley said, positioning the wheelchair and locking it as I transfer from the wheelchair to the driver's seat.

"He must of stuffed it under the seat." I said, faking a search for stuff that doesn't exist.

Four ambulances pull into the ER parking lot.

"Oh my. They may need my help Officer Otis. Can you stay here until I get back please?"

"Yeah, go handle your business. I'm still looking for my stuff."

I watch Ashley hurry to one of the ambulances, get instructions from one of the doctors coming out of Trinity and rush alongside one of the gurneys going into ER. Now's my chance. My run in with her was much longer than it should've been.

Starting the patrol car engine, I gingerly drive out of the ER parking lot, hoping I don't crash this damned thing. Also hoping April and the officer are still asleep.

It's tricky driving with my left foot, but I've driven six blocks without incident. So far so good. Ten or so more miles left. Slow and steady, no sirens no lights, don't draw attention.

Needing to hear if they're tracking me, I turn on the police radio. After a few minutes and more miles, there's no mention of me or Trinity hospital. In front of me I see apartment buildings sprouting out of the trees. I'm near Seawell State Park and home, relief. Maybe.

Driving the patrol car into the parking lot spooks the few standing outside, inside.

"Go ahead you fuckers, go inside." I said, parking the car, not wanting anyone seeing me dressed up like a cop and shit anyway.

Getting my crutches from the car, I begin my journey up those hated steps. This time no Carlito or Andrew for help, just crutches. However, after a few flights up, it isn't that bad. Made it up all flights without trouble, or sweat. Weird.

Playing around, swinging my body back and forth on the crutches, I swing my happy ass to my apartment door. I then realize I don't have my apartment keys, again. Luckily there's an extra key I placed behind the loose brick next to my door. Couldn't reveal that when Carlito and Andrew helped me earlier. Retrieving the key, I open the door and make a beeline to my hallway closet.

"There you are." I said, smiling at my extra prosthetic, the good one, in front of my old original prosthetic that no longer fits. Snatching it up, I hop into my bedroom to get some clothes and shoes.

"Raccoon. Funny." I said, to myself, checking out my bucket, mop, lemon funk mixed sheets and cleanser leaning against the wall.

My body's not drained and I'm not tired, or worn out.

"Crazy."

I reach over and turn on my clock radio. A commercial airs as I unbutton this heavy ass dark blue police shirt, wanting to hear any news about Trinity hospital or what happened last night at Club 898.

"Another one? Shit." I mumble, as another commercial airs.

Cops clothes are off me now. More commercials air as I shove my prosthetic leg into the pants leg of my own pants. National news airs, then the local news airs while tying my shoe, "Last night was a nightmare in downtown Baltimore. Club 898, a popular downtown hot spot, became a house of horrors as some type of animal got into the club, attacking and killing many of the club patrons, and seriously wounding others. Central City Police confirmed there were 28 people killed in this attack. Included in that number was noted bounty hunter Shaun Fuller……"

"What?!"

"…No word yet on what type of animal this was and no reports of any animal or animals escaping from the City Zoo."

"Oh my God. Shaun's dead?" There must be some mistake!"

I look on my dresser and nightstand for my cell to call Kari but it's not there. I'm fully pieced together, so I jump up to get to my landline to call Kari.

"Hello?" Kari answers, half asleep.

"Kari, this is Cocamoe. I just heard something on the radio about Shaun and Club 898."

"Cocamoe? Aren't you in the hospital?"

"Never mind that, Kari. What's this about Shaun!"

"Cocamoe…...Shaun's dead. Happened at Club 898….."

"Dead! What the hell happened?"

Emotion bursts from Kari, between her tears and heavy breathing I make out small bits.

"This….thing….. attacked everyone, this….animal. We thought it killed you…..Shaun went back ……..then alley….Shaun dead…..they took you to hospital."

"Kari. I've got to go, sorry." I said, pressing down on the switch hook. Slamming the phone receiver hard onto the base, my head pounds. Sweat froths on my weakening hot body, dropping me to the ground.

"I don't believe it. Shaun is dead."

Laying on the floor sweating, hot and feeling sick, flashes of something like this from last night flutter in my head. My stump hurts, prosthetic tightens while more local news airs.

"This just in, famed local bounty hunter, Joseph Cocamoe, has reportedly escaped police custody from Trinity Hospital late this evening. He is considered armed and dangerous. If you know his whereabouts or see Mr. Cocamoe, please call 911."

Hearing this new shit is making the torture in my body subside. The sweating stops and my leg feels fine, no swelling or tightness. Don't know why or what this crazy shit is but I do know I don't like it one damned bit.

"Gotta get outta here before they come for me!" I said, pulling myself up off the floor.

I go back to my closet getting my other gun. Snub nose .38, small but powerful. I'm taking the old bulky prosthetic too, just in case.
Hustling down the stairs, I slow down, staring at the patrol car.

"I can't roll out of here with that car."

That's when I see Andrew's mint condition, electric blue 75 Cadillac Coupe DeVille.

"Shit, I'll borrow Andrew's ride. He won't mind. But first, I've got to get something from the patrol car." I said, going to the patrol car, opening the trunk to take out the universal slim-jim. Easily, I unlock his Caddie and throw in my leg. Of course, the Caddie's alarm screams out as I'm jimmying the ignition. Takes me ten seconds to replace that mechanical whining with the smooth deep purr of this beauty's engine.

My admiration of Andrew's car is cut short by Andrew himself flying out of his apartment to his car and me. Smirking, I shift in reverse, smoothly turn the car around and speed away. The rear view mirror shows Andrew arms waving in the air, his mouth flailing about with no sound. This machine's awesome heartbeat drowns it out.

On to find Hassan. Guess I'll go to last spot Shaun and I saw him. Just that small ass little thought brings images of Shaun. I've no time for this shit. Gotta concentrate on my task at hand.

"Fuck! 5-0!"

I just passed a patrol car going in the other direction. Checking the rear view mirror I see it hasn't turned around. It's about 100 yards from where we initially passed. I check again to see if it turns around and it does. I'm going 5 miles below the posted speed. So speeding ain't the issue. I'm about 10 miles away from my complex, so maybe they're responding to Andrew's call. Damn, it's getting closer. I pull my gun from belt, placing it on the passenger seat. To hide it I pull down the middle armrest, just in case.

He's directly behind me now, the sweating starts again, this time my head hurts like a motherfucker as my stump rapidly throbs against my prosthetic.

Slowing down Andrew's Caddie, the officer slows down too and turns on his patrol car's blue flashing lights. Taking deep slow breaths is all I can do to keep from passing out. I slide down the window to get some air, when my lucky ass sees the patrol car turnaround, headed in the opposite direction. With the Caddie completely stopped, my inner voice repeats 'calm down asshole, calm down asshole.'

Mixed in with my deep breaths come thoughts of April and finding Hassan. 'Inhale asshole, exhale asshole'. I'm still not understanding the changes going on with my body. After I find Hassan I'll go visit Dr. Seti. First things first, find Hassan.

I take another deep breath, when there's a knock on my window. Flinching, I look to my left before reaching for the gun. Good thing I did.

"You okay sir?" the voice outside Andrew's car asked.

Standing next to the Caddie is a Metro Police Officer. Shit. They're just like the damned State Troopers, same authority, just different stupid ass uniforms. I take a quick look in my rear view mirror and see it's only him. He's alone and no Baltimore City Police around. Why didn't I hear or smell this shithead coming up on me?

"You okay sir?" the Metro Police Officer, asked again.

"Yes. I'm okay officer, long shift at work."

The Metro Police Officer stares at me, looks around the interior of the Caddie then steps back. I thought he saw my leg, but he said nothing.

"I saw BCP tailing you then they turned around. Now you sure you're ok sir?"

"Yeah, just needed a little break before getting home."

"Be careful sir. Get some rest and watch out for that big bad wolf. By the way, nice Caddie." he said.

"Thanks. No worries about any wolf here. I left my picnic baskets at home with grandma anyway." I said, thinking that this wolf thing has everyone on edge. Metro Officer didn't ask for my license, registration or anything. Guess he didn't want to be distracted while on this lonely ass wooded road and have some make-believe wolf attack him.

He smiles, looks me over again then heads back to his patrol car pretty quickly. I stay parked in the spot I'm in waiting for him to pull off ahead of me, but he's just sitting there. Talking into his car radio microphone.
Staying glued to his every move, my body tenses up, again. When he turns on his patrol car's lights, reverses his car and turns around. I calm down, a bit. He must've gotten another call.

"I hope I'm done with all this cop bullshit, ain't even gotten outta this damned park."

Andrew's analog car clock does work, it's 5:49 a.m.. The sun'll be rising in a couple of hours. After a few minutes of decompressing myself, I put the Caddie in drive and head to East Baltimore. Milton and Monument Street, last place I...we, saw Hassan.

Meanwhile, in his office at Northwest District, Detective Norris is trying to piece together some of the events from previous days. Elderly couple massacred in Seawell State Park at night. Well known bounty hunter found in Seawell State Park next morning, naked, without leg and unsure how he got there. Blood of bounty hunter matches blood found at elderly couple's crime scene. There are mass killings, including Shaun, at local nightclub. Same bounty hunter found in alley behind nightclub, naked, legless and unconscious.

Detective Norris sits at his desk repeatedly looking over his notes, when there's a knock on the door.

"Sorry sir. Got a report from Central City that Cocamoe left the hospital. He subdued a Central City Officer and took his car." an officer reports.

Detective Norris grins, jumps up and snatches his jacket while running out the door. The officer stands rigid against the wall, getting out of the way.

"Also sir, the animal guys from the zoo said all animals are accounted for. Park Rangers called too, said no such animal exists in any park in Maryland. And the forensic guys found several wolf hairs at the Seawell State Park elderly couple crime scene and inside club 898!" the officer shouts, to the running detective.

"Put that report on my desk!" Norris shouts back.
Trinity Hospital is jumping. April is awake, been that way for a few hours.

She's pissed that the police were guarding the room and now Cocamoe's gone. Officers, doctors and Lucy are asking April multiple questions about what took place in the room and she's not being cooperative at all.

"Ask the beat downed cop, not me." April repeats.

"April. They're just trying to help" Lucy said, trying to calm April down.

"Yeah, I know. I've got to go to the bathroom." April said, feigning sincerity.

She heads towards the bathroom door then notices no one is by the front door. She rushes to get out but is stopped by Detective Laboo coming into the room.

"Glad you're still here ma'am. I've got so many questions for you." he said, escorting her back inside.

10 ARABBERS

In my drive to Hassan's area, I see the dregs of humanity mixed in with the honest hard working people. Some, on bus stops going to work, others using bus stops as temporary homes. It's 8 a.m., I've driven around the East side of Baltimore for 2 hours and no sign of Hassan. I thought Arabbers started real early in the morning to sell their stuff. The main hangout in this area is the hospital, world famous William Frances Middleton Hospital. I assumed nurses, doctors, hospital employees and people from the neighborhood would be out getting breakfast, fruit and other crap from an Arabber or Hassan. There are no Arabbers, no damned Hassan or many people out here, so I ride around some more, looking.

Some of the row houses in this area are impeccable, others are shitty and decrepit. Some folk take great pride in their houses. Spraying the filth off the sidewalks, their pearly white marble step, with the black streaks, and those painted white truck tire planters, with hoses.

Just then, a swarm of students, doctors or interns, come out of one of the hospital buildings. A quick thought enters my head, 'go inside and have them take a look at me'. That's erased when I see a familiar face. Can't place the name, but the face I can't forget. Two large gold plated teeth next to several missing teeth, small scar on his left cheek, probably from a knife fight and thick ass eyeglasses that are too big for his thin face. I pull up alongside him as he is leans against the building the interns are coming out of.

"Yo. My man, you seen Hassan the Arabber today?" I yell out.

"Don't wrap to 5-0." the gold tooth guy yells back, lowering his head.

"Do I look like 5-0?"

The gold toothed guy leans his head down further, his red baseball cap almost falls off his tiny head as he looks at me over his coke bottle glasses.

"You look like that motherfucker on the news that made a break outta

79

Trinity!"

So. He isn't as dumb as he looks.

"Dude. I need to find Hassan pretty bad. I need his help."

The gold toothed guy gets silent, still checking me out when he sucks his tooth, never really moving his body from the dusty red brick wall.

"Wolfe street!" he yells, pushing his glasses back onto his face with his left hand.

"Thanks my man." I shout, driving away.

At the corner, there's a stop sign where I need to make a right turn. I hesitate then break into laughter.

"Here I am looking for a crazy old dude that said 'I'm one with the wolf' and his ass lives on Wolfe Street."

Making the turn heading towards Wolfe Street, a faint animal smell arouses me. I've smelled it before, but can't pinpoint what it is or where it's coming from. The smell a pungent mixture of manure, watermelon, strawberries and collards gets stronger. It's Hassan's horse.

Slowing the Caddie, I see a sturdy makeshift barn/stall behind a house on the corner end of Wolfe and Preston Streets. The horse is very agitated and his loud whining forces Hassan out of the house. He stops at the top step, gives me a quick glance then limps hurriedly to his horse. I park the Caddie and get out. My arousal of his horse's smell really weird's me out, but I lean against the car, to wait patiently for Hassan. Lord knows I don't want to agitate him too.

"So. You tracked me down. Good." Hassan said, coming from around the corner where I can hear that his horse has calmed down

"What up, Hassan. I need to talk to you." I said.

"Come in. Come in quick." Hassan said, leading me into his house.

Pausing, slightly, I enter his brilliantly lit foyer. Above me, where the ceiling would normally be, sunlight bounces warmly off the canary yellow paint through the large window, inviting me in.

"Come. This way." Hassan said, getting my attention back on him.

I'm really liking the architecture when I stop at the doorway that exits the foyer. Long thin strands of rope hang from the top of the doorway to the floor itself. They're slightly moving from Hassan already walking through them.

"It's just Cannabis rope, won't kill you." Hassan said.

"I know. Can we smoke this later?"

"No."

I follow into the other room but not before I take a big sniff of the hanging cannabis rope.

"Nice smell." I mutter.

This room, sorta what I expected from an old dude from Africa. Huge orange, red, tan and kente cloth pillows on the floor atop a thick oriental rug that covers ¾ of the room. An oversized wooden chair with a wide back, aerated with medium holes. Walls in this room are dull blood red, a big contrast to the foyer. Several African masks adorn one wall, along with animal skins. Various pieces of wood, a small single shelf and small pieces of animal bones are on another wall. The other two are barren.

"Sit." Hassan said, pointing to a large orange pillow in front of the wooden chair.

"Why I get the pillow and not the chair? I am disabled you know."

"Sit!" Hassan shouts.

I sit, very cautiously onto the large pillow.

"I hope this doesn't bother your nose too much." Hassan said, as he fires up several sticks of pomegranate incense.

"Look old man. I want to know what you know about what's going on with me."

"I already told you. You are one with the wolf."

"What the fuck does that mean, old man!"

Hassan smiles, sits back further in his wooden chair.

"Plain and simple, "Mannix" (70's detective reference). You are a werewolf. You got bitten by one before you killed it so now you're one."

"As I told you and Shaun before, I ain't no damned werewolf. Those things don't exist!"

"Club 898 and all those other killings. That was you." Hassan calmly said.

"That's crazy. News reports say those people were shredded, massacred by a huge animal!" I said.

"You weren't a person at the time. You were the beast."

"What's this beast, werewolf shit you keep saying?"

Hassan rises slowly from his chair.

"Shaun, your partner. You killed him when you turned into the beast. You can't control it nor remember when you turn into it. Anything can set it off. Stress, anger, passion, fright......"

I jump up, stumbling towards Hassan's face.

"Anger triggers it? Like now? Well, asshole, I'm still human and I do really want to rip your damned mouth off!" I scream.

Hassan leans back, squints his eyes and begins chanting an African chant. My right eye tilts (by itself?) upward at his strange reaction. I quickly take a look at my arms and nothing has changed, I'm still human. Anger hasn't changed me into any beast, not that I really wanted it to. Just glad to prove him wrong.

"What's the deal with that chant shit? Does it stop me from changing into this werewolf thing!?" I ask, easing away from Hassan's face.

"No. It soothes your temperament." Hassan said, walking away from his wooden chair and me. He goes to that small shelf embedded in the wall where there's a small box. Hassan pulls out that damned amulet that he tried to give me earlier.

"This time, you will take it. Trust me, it will help. Here too is a key to my house. You may need a place to stay after your escape from the hospital." Hassan said, handing me the amulet and the key.

"This shit again? Ok old man, I'm gonna take your amulet just to shut you up. Your house key, I probably really do need that." I said, taking both items, placing the amulet in my pocket without really looking at it.

"You may want to hide your car and get some rest."

"Yeah, ok." I said, leaving the blood red room, feeling more fucked up and confused than before as I head to the car.

Instead of moving the car I open Andrew's trunk, hoping his anal nature wouldn't fail me. In the rear of the trunk I see the folded up car cover. Unrolling it to cover the car, I feel bitter. If I had stayed my ass home instead of chasing Randy through the stupid ass woods this shit wouldn't be happening to me. I need to get myself fixed.

When the car's fully covered I head back into Hassan's. Finding him asleep in the wooden chair in the blood red room, I take heed to him telling me to rest. I get down onto the floor without taking myself apart and lay my head on the large orange pillow. I try to sleep but can't, too much going on in my head.

Hearing something moving around in another room I open my eyes and I don't see Hassan.

"He's a stealthy old fuck." I said, smiling.

Soothing me is the smell of food, Hassan's cooking. Naturally, I follow the smell.

There's a table made of chipped battered driftwood connected to hinges on the lime green wall. On the table is a wooden bowl with slices of peaches, bread, honey and rice for me, I guess. Hassan's sitting on a stool at the table. He has a wooden bowl too, but his has stuff that looks like mud, but smells like apples. He points for me to sit down.

We eat quietly with our hands, but I have so many questions.

"What time is it?" I ask, chewing on a piece of bread dipped in honey.

"Time for supper. You didn't sleep, rested body a long time but not your mind, food will help rest mind." Hassan said, placing a glob of his food in his mouth.

"Hassan, if I am a so-called werewolf and I kill people, why aren't you afraid of me?"

"Death, no matter what form it takes, does not frighten me."

"Yeah…..ok, so If I'm a werewolf and I change from what I am now into this huge killing beast, when I change back to human, can I stay human?"

"Yes."

Grinning, I scoop up some rice and honey.

"Really, how?"

"When you die."

Good thing my food was swallowed.

"When I die huh, you for real or what?"

"I never lie, no need to."

"So, let me get this right. You, say I'm a werewolf and I kill and eat people?"

"Correct."

"Ok, now the only way for me to not be a werewolf ever is for me to die?"

"Correct."

I re-adjust myself on the stool while looking around my surroundings then straight back to Hassan.

"According to my man Shaun, the only way to kill a werewolf, which I obviously ain't, is to burn it or behead it."

"Correct again."

"Damn. I'd hate to be a werewolf." I said, chewing on the last piece of bread and honey, taking the amulet from my pocket.

"What you say this thing is again, Wepwawet or something?"

"Wepwawet, the Egyptian Wolf God. Its power will prevent you from changing into the beast." Hassan said, getting up from the table and limping out of the kitchen.

"Okay, awesome." I mumble, trying not to laugh again at all he's saying to me.

"Hassan. What's the deal with calling me and Shaun the names of old police characters from TV?"

"No real reason. Just one of my old man things."

"You're lucky I like and respect you. I'm going to go along with your horror story until all this crazy shit with Shaun and the club is over." I said, stretching and yawning.

Hassan limps back into the kitchen, carrying a candle holder with a lit candle. With a stern decisive motion, his index finger beckons me to follow him. We both amble a few feet when Hassan stops.

"You sleep here, purity will make your mind sleep." Hassan said.

Walking into the newly lit room, I see it's bare. Pale white walls, no paintings or masks hang here, no furniture, only a long orange and brown worn out thin African blanket and a small red pillow. Hassan starts to leave the room, forcing me out of his way. As I take in the emptiness of my new room, Hassan turns to me, bows, then hands me the candle holder.

"Wait a minute old man! Where do you sleep? You know, in case I need more questions answered."

"Tonight, in the stable. Your presence here upsets my horse. However, it's my duty to care for life, yours and his." He said, vanishing into the darkness.

Shrugging my shoulders, I set the candle holder on the floor and ease myself down onto the thin ass blanket, feeling my sleepiness. Initially I was going to take off my prosthetic but decided to keep it on, again, just in case. Sleeping with it on is kinda uncomfortable, a lot more different than just laying down with it on, like I did earlier.

I unholster my gun, unsheathe my knife, take Hassan's keys and amulet out of my pocket and place all next to one another until I pick up the amulet. I want to get a closer look at it. Dark hard wood figurine of a creature with the head of a wolf but the body of a man. The amulet isn't too detailed, rather plain actually. About 5 inches in length and 1 inch in thickness but relatively light. It's holding a staff close to its body. Atop this staff is an Ankh; Kemet's, or Ancient Egyptian, symbol of eternal life. I know this because April and I were looking at wedding rings when she saw one with the Ankh symbol and fell in love with it.

Too late at night for me to be doing all this thinking. I place the amulet around my neck, not acknowledging that werewolf crap, just being cautious. I blow out the candle and lay my head on that small ass pillow. Hopefully I'll have a safe sleep and wake up in the same damned place. Connected.

11 SENSORY OVERLOAD

Morning does come. Hearing Hassan connecting the cart to his horse, I lay there. Gingerly, I move my right leg because it feels heavy and slightly sore. Good. That's an indication that it's still here. Easing up from my waist, I stretch to get the kinks out. Glad the room is still pale, blanket still thin, orange and brown. Pillow's red, amulet still around my neck, keys on floor next to candle, gun and knife there as well. Relieved this is where I went to sleep and also where I wake the hell up.

Without notice, the crashing of sounds bum rushes me; Hassan talking to his horse, the horse and the cart clip clopping down the alley, clashes with the neighborhood chatter and cars motoring along. Then the overlap of sounds cease.

"Comes and goes. Comes and goes. I've got to remember to go see Dr. Seti about this shit."

Reaching down to pick up those sets of keys, my gun and the knife, I take a look at my reflection in my knife's shiny blade..

"Not bad. Not bad at all for a shithead that's suppose to be a werewolf." I said, playfully howling into the air.

Now comes the get off the floor part. I roll myself onto my hands and knees, pushing myself up with my real leg. Balancing my body until I can get my prosthetic leg up under myself then stand up. Great piece of exercise.

"I wonder if Hassan has more rooms in this house?" I ask myself, straightening my clothes and my body.

Leaving the pale room, I walk back into the blood red room with all the pillows, burned out incense and wooden chair. The only other doors I see are the one leading to the foyer and the one leading to the kitchen. A faint coconut smell, slow grinds with the hanging cannabis rope aroma in my mind. Inhaling deeply, I notice another shelf on the blood red wall. This one has books on it. Walking over to check them out I step on one laying on the floor. It's title reads, "Wolf, The Beast Within Us All."

"Interesting. This is what Hassan was probably reading this morning or he left it on the floor for me to see and read it."

I thought about reading it but instead place it on the shelf. My true mission now is eating. Hassan has food but I need something more substantial and fresh. Anyway, I need fresh air. Going out is probably stupid but sometimes the best place to hide is right where people can see you, military training kicking in. I walk through the cannabis curtain into the foyer and peer out the door, making sure there are no police outside of Hassan's house. Don't see any and I feel it's safe to leave so I leave, making sure to lock his door behind me. One step down off the porch, my nose and ears are attacked, again. Smells and sounds are more intense. I fall hard, back into the closed front door covering my nose and trying to wrap my left arm around my ears. The smell of horse shit, car exhaust, people's body odor, rotten fruit and others odors mesh with the sounds of car tires rubbing the road, people yelling from a distance, traffic horns, cats hissing and other shit I definitely couldn't hear before. Once more, without warning, everything goes away, all the smells and the sounds, gone. The only smell remaining is someone cooking food.

Slightly bent over from the pain of the noise and smell smorgasbord, I collect myself as best I can. Not a soul paid any attention to my damned struggle. No time to get pissed off at society, my stomach grumbles as that smell of food gets stronger.

A few blocks down the street I see several people coming out of a building with brown paper bags enclosed in white plastic bags. I smell bacon, eggs, hash browns, pancakes and syrup. Walking in the direction of those smells, I see more people coming out of this small neighborhood diner named "Gwenie's".

In opening the door, you'd thought I was transformed into the Old West. Major cliche', but all chatter inside the diner stops, all eyes turn to me, and I swear the music stops too.

'What the fuck y'all looking at!' was what I wanted to yell out, but I stay calm and rational, thinking 'they ain't never seen me before in their hood.' My mind is jarred when I hear this deep baritone voice ring out.

"May I help you, sir?"

Turning to that voice, I see what stands is a mountain of a man, dressed in a black waist length kitchen smock worn over a red pleated dress, cut just above his knees. His dark red lipstick straggles both lips into one. Black blush and purple eyeshadow is overwhelmingly splattered onto his light brown cherub face, covering five o'clock shadow.

"I ain't on the menu dammit!" This man shouts, as customers in the diner start laughing at my gaze.

"My bad. I'm just very hungry and when I turn and see you, I'm like wow, awesome." I said softly and sweetly, noticing the large 'Gwenie' tattoo on his massive forearm.

"What'll you have? And 'yes' I am Gwenie." he said, in a softer tone.

"I'll take 20 pieces of raw bacon and one huge cup of coffee." I said, just now realizing I just asked for 'raw' food.

"Raw bacon? Twenty pieces? Look, son of a bitch, this ain't no damned supermarket. Get your weird ass outta here!" Gwenie yells, picking up his meat cleaver.

"Hold the hell up! I got no beef with you. Calm down, my bad. Please cook them. A slip of the tongue. Calm down." I said, backing away from the counter, amid more laughter.

Gwenie relaxes a little and retreats, embedding the cleaver hard into the counter.

"Twenty pieces, right?" Gwenie asks.

"Yes sir, ma'am. Yes, 20 pieces." I said, trying to be as neutral as possible.

Gwenie smiles.

"Take a seat, this will take a while"

A few seats are available at the counter. The weathered red leather vintage bar stool in the middle of the counter is my pic. A good arm's distance away from Gwenie, who throws all of my bacon onto the grill causing smoke to fill up the counter area. The ear piercing sizzling is damn near deafening to me, so I get u. Moving further down the counter, walking pass the cronies at the counter, I see up on the wall a television and a payphone further back. A pay phone does exist.

"Hey Gwenie. Does that thing work?" I yell, pointing at the payphone.

Gwenie looks down at his penis, smiles, then yells back,

"Hell yeah it works!"

Customers crack up laughing again.

"Your pay phone. Just your pay phone."

"Yeah that works too. Ungrateful asshole!"

Making my way to the pay phone, I see it's in a darker area of the diner, perfect. It takes coins and all I have is a ten spot. Was on my way back up to Gwenie to get change when I see what's on the TV. It's on mute but has the closed captions running along the bottom of the screen. The news is on, just great. Captions read:

'Still no word on who or what attacked and killed 28 patrons inside popular downtown nightclub Club 898. There were no cameras inside or outside of the club but eyewitnesses state it's definitely a WHAT and not a who that did these killings.'

There's some chatter from Gwennie's patrons concerning the craziness they see and read about Club 898, not too much though, especially not from the elders there. They tend not to talk too loud about shit that seems too real to be anything but strange. Suddenly my picture's slapped up on the screen.

"Shit."

The diner's front door opens and two of Baltimore's Finest enter.

"Hold your horses guys, your order may be delayed 'cause I got a BIG FUCKING order of bacon and it's cooking now!" Gwenie said, before the officers can say anything.

She more than likely looked in my direction but I was no longer there, the back door was opened to help with ventilation and my exit. I'm more watchful and hungrier in my walk back to Hassan's house.

A new food smell tingles my nose, fresher meat. It's fish, fresh from the Bay. One of Hassan's neighbors left their cooler of the morning catch in the rear of their pickup. No one's around, so I grab the cooler. Hustling to the alley leading to the stable, I hear yelling and cursing about their catch being stolen, but I had already reached my destination, and too hungry to take the cooler into the house.

Within seconds I'm crouched as low to the ground as I can inside the stable, ripping the top off the cooler, devouring the raw fish. Several violent crude harsh chomps and I stop, looking at what the hell I'm doing. Guts, blood, ice and pieces of fish are scattered all over the hay, and horse shit riddled stable floor. My hand holds the bloody half of a fish which I throw to the stable floor.

"What the fuck is wrong with me?" I cry out, kicking the cooler over.

My attention centers on fast footsteps coming down the alley. Gathering myself, I quickly slip into Hassan's house and peek out of a small window. Two men arrive, looking down at the turned over cooler and their mangled fish. Their eyes search up and down the alley, but never at Hassan's house. In an instant they sprint down the alley looking for their thief.

Pulling away from the small window, I realize I'm in the kitchen. Not noticing from my time in here before, there's peeling pink stucco paint on the ceiling with signs of water damage. Hassan's driftwood table is unhinged from the wall. On top of the table is a small plate of fruit and a hot plate. Left of the table is a small brown refrigerator, similar to the one I had in college at good ole Cheyney University of Pennsylvania, the oldest HBCU in America. Strange, not to see an oven in the kitchen, just the hotplate.

Several books are on top of that small fridge, all with titles written in foreign languages except one. 'Werewolves, Never Change'. The title makes me laugh, so I have to check it out. Wiping fish residue off my hands onto my pants, I pick up the book. First page has some handwriting on it, in German. It translates: 'Hassan. Defeater of my many demons. Adolph.'

"Yeah right."

Nevertheless, I turn to the next page.

The first sentence reads: 'A Werewolf's only pleasure is to kill, eat, kill, eat, then sleep.' Again I laugh, continuing to read while walking, finding myself in the blood red room with the huge wooden chair and pillow. Taking a seat to read more, my hunger has left.

Time passes. Hassan's still out, and this book's really pulled me in. Before closing it, I re-read the handwritten note on the first page and the title. There's some crazy werewolf occult shit written in this book. Gotta get my head straight though. Today is Saturday and I haven't forgotten about capturing Edgar.

My body's pretty stiff from sitting and reading. Stretching long and hard with a few waist bends has me thinking of April, Kari and Shaun. I want to reach out to April but I know she's being watched and I'm quite sure her phone is bugged.

Almost done, my blood's flowing really good. I'm thinking clearer of my next move before I leave. My first clear move is to make sure everything in Hassan's house is just the way he left. My second move was to go to Andrew's car to get my other prosthetic from the front seat, but too many people are out and about. Instead, I take advantage of a taxi coming down the street.

"Where to sir?"

"33rd and Greenmount."

Taxi's clock reads 6:30 a.m.. I have more than enough time to do what I need to do before getting to Edgar.

"Driver. Run me to Cheraton Road in Cherry Hill first."

"Cherry Hill, yes sir!."

The Cabbie's enthusiasm comes from more money added to my fare, while mine comes from the fact that it's where April lives.

Ten minutes into the ride, new thoughts run a relay with my old thoughts; Shaun's death, the night that wolf-thing attacked me and Randy, me naked in the park, those words from Hassan, his books and this damned amulet. Feeling the taxi slowing down, I see we're on Cheraton Road, two blocks from April's house. I also see two unmarked police cars on her street, one up the block, the other a few feet from her house.

"Keep going, she's not home." I said.

As the taxi rides pass the first officer I sink my head lower inside the cab, slightly rising as we ride in front of her house. There are two more officers, in the street alleyway, waiting.

"I hope you're not trying to rob me."

"Naw man, you're good. I'm sleepy. Head on up to 33rd and Greenmount."

Taking a look at the meter and the time; $15.75 and 7:15 p.m., I figure we'll get to Greenmount around 8'ish.

Taxi makes a left turn on Terra Firma, setting to leave Cherry Hill. Dogfight ain't till 1:00 a.m., so I've got time. I lay my head back to see if I can get some real rest. Once again, I can't. The street lights sync with the cabs movement, flashing fast and chaotic, reminding me of Club 898. My right arm starts shaking lightly, then damn near uncontrollable, like I'm having a fucking seizure. This shit's new, with the old other shit following; body getting warm, right stump flinching. The taxi comes to a stop, as does the shit discombobulating my body. A little dazed, I look out the window to see where we are.

"Here we are sir, 33rd and Greenmount." the cabbie blurts out.

The dashboard clock reads 7:55 p.m.. My timing was pretty accurate. Cabbie stopped next to the gas station a few feet away from the nightclub/bar Shelby's. A spot I usually go to for a few drinks, but with my face all over the airwaves, now it's not a good idea.

Paying the cabbie, I get out and head over to Cray-Cray's sub shop, half a block up from Shelby's. Through the big picture windows of Cray-Cray's I only see two people in there along with two employees. The two customers are more than likely either drunk or high, so they won't notice me. I'll take my chances with the employees.

"Evening sir. How may I help you?" the more than enthusiastic, cute cashier asks, as I enter.

"Evening. Yeah, cheese-steak, medium rare, large order of fries and a chocolate shake." I said, eyeing an empty booth way in the back, and remembering what happened at Gwennie's when I ordered raw food.

"Cheese-steak medium rare. What you want on it?"

"Onions, lettuce, extra hots, mustard and pepper."

I've got about four hours to waste. I'll use this time to make up a plan to get Edgar and the 100% likelihood that I'll have to fight his boys to get him out of there. Giving Edgar's wanted poster the once over again, the word 'Alive' rings over and over in my head.

"Here you go sir. Bloody cheese-steak, bad breath clusters, fake money and lead me into hell spices. Fries and chocolate shake." the cashier/waitress said, bringing me my food.

"Real creative with your choice of words young lady."

"Overnight shift. I have to be, with the craz...... Can I get you anything else?"

"Nope. I'm good."

She gives me a funny look before heading back to the front of the sub shop.

"Yeah, ok." I said, dismissing her look. More interested in my food, for right now.

Biting into my sub, blood juices from the cow slightly dull the explosions from the extra hots, mustard, peppers and onions. My chewing, hard vigorous and hot, is cooled a bit by my chocolate shake, but water is needed.

I get up rushing to the counter, covering my partially opened mouth. My dumb ass, still chewing, swallows, bringing tears to my eyes as snot trickles from my nose. Before I could say anything to the cashier/waitress, she points to a large cup filled with water and ice next to her register. Awesome. After my brief respite, I turn to her nodding my approval. While taking another sip, I begin checking her out. Not bad, nice tight little body.

"Really appreciate that sweetheart. Guess my food concoction was spicier than expected."

"My pleasure." she giggles.

There's only one person left in Cray-Cray's, a tall fat drunk dude, playing keno. The other employee left. In the air is a beautiful pungent aroma coming from the cashier/waitress direction. Here I go smelling shit that probably shouldn't be smelled, fucking crazy. Right now though, I like it. That smell is her, telling me she's as horny as I am. She smiles, noticing how I'm looking at her. I try halting myself but my libido takes over. Haven't felt this way since April.

The cashier/waitress's short auburn twisted locs, dark ebony glowing skin and palm sized breasts have me more than ready. She's comes from behind the counter. Without waiting, I snatch her arm pulling her closer to me. The smell of her desire mingled with the smell of bubble bath, onions, meat, and strawberry lip gloss. My right hand, now firmly planted on her small tight ass, has me growl slightly, matching her whimper.

"Dammit. Almost had that son of a bitch!" shouts the keno playing drunk.

She pulls away from me hard.

"We can't do nothing here. It's almost time for Linda's shift and for Leroy to come back."

"You're right. Way in the back or a closet is better." I said, grabbing her thin hips.

"Nooooo….." She said.

Leaning down to kiss her, the front door opens and I release her. Several customers along with her two co-workers walk in.

"Yo. What up Tami, girl." the female co-worker said, looking at the drunk keno player then me.

"Hey Linda. What up Leroy." Tami said, trying to fix her clothes.

Leroy has a big smile on his face until he sees I hadn't left. Tami is on the other side of the counter. I head to my back booth and sub with my cup of water in hand. Leroy, never saying a word to me or Tami, peers curiously at us both. I don't need any confrontation before my getting of Edgar, so I sit down and continue on what's left of my sub and them cold ass fries.

I hear Tami and Linda whispering to one another as they walk to the front office. Linda asks Tami what's going on.

"Girl….I was gonna rock his world till you two and them other motherfuckers came in."

"He is kinda hot. Maybe we should both do him." Linda said.

Smiling, I continue eating, happy knowing Tami does have a dark side. This new found super damn hearing and smelling ain't so bad. Just glad they're not running into each other like before.

More people come into Cray-Cray's, ordering food and drinks. It's 9:30 p.m., according to the clock on the wall. Tami walks from the front office area, smiling in my direction. I shake my head at what I almost did to that girl. Never done any shit like that before. All's well that ends well, I guess. Going to try and get some sleep before getting Edgar, but I have one more thing to do. Most of the customers are outside smoking and talking, Linda is watching the drunk keno player and Leroy's in the back. I can safely approach Tami again.

"Hey Tami. Let me get one of those pay as you go cells and a card please?"

"Which one?"

"Any kind except a flip piece of shit."

Her eyes twinkle. Tami pulls a twenty dollar phone card out of the card holder then a slim streamlined cell phone from the wall behind her. She rings up the items.

"Sixty-nine ninety nine." she giggles.

"Great number." I said, grinning.

Handing her the money, I lightly caress her hand with her slowly pulling back, sighing. I'm only getting this phone because it's untraceable. It will enable me to check on April and it has an alarm, to wake me for Edgar.

Leroy comes out from the back, cuts his eye at me. Linda, walking to the front door to let someone know their order is ready, checks me out with this sheepish grin on her face. My winking at her, irritates Tami, making her yank the cell package from my hand.

"What's up with that?" Tami shouts.

"Calm down baby. There's enough for the both of y'all."

"Yeah, whatever!" she huffs.

Tami slams my change, cell phone package and card on the counter. Now I'm irritated.

Forcibly enclosing my hand around her dainty wrist makes her squeal. She tries pulling away, but can't. Squeezing tighter, her eyes puff up with fear. I feel and smell her insides churn.

Sensing Leroy coming towards me, I release her.

Cocamoe's unaware that the Wepwawet amulet is working. Although, the beast inside him is getting more powerful and savage, making the battle to contain this evil more difficult.

"No harm done. Just playing with the young lady." I said, sneering at Leroy.

Linda rushes up, embracing Tami while I back further away from them. Leroy parts his lips like he's going to say something until I look his way. Customers coming back inside ignore or really didn't see our little interaction. I go back to my booth, take a bite out of my sub and start
    unwrapping my new cell.

After way too many stupid ass minutes of ripping through the shrink wrap package I get to the phone. Plugging it in for activation, I fiddle around with the phone and the prompts instructions from the phones service desk.

"Wow. That was quick." I said, looking at the confirmation that the damned cell is now activated on the display window.

It's 10:25 p.m. I dial April's cell to check on her. Her phone rings, and rings. After the seventh ring, her answering machine kicks in. I quickly disconnect, not wanting to leave a message.

Why didn't she pick up? Maybe, she doesn't recognize the number? She knows I'm on the run and would try different means to contact her. Maybe she just ain't in? Where in the hell would she be on a Saturday night at 10:30 without me? Kari. Yeah she's over Kari's crib, keeping her company. That's where she'd better be anyway.

Exhaling deeply, I calm myself before calling Kari's crib to check. Looking around the sub shop, I realize that I didn't get any of those weird sweaty sensations or any throbbing in my right stump because April didn't answer. I pat my right pant leg where Hassan's amulet rests, unsure if I believe in what he said or if this whole thing is one wide awake nightmare.

"Better get some sleep. I'm not calling Kari, I do hope April's ok. Alarm is set for 11:45 p.m., dogfights at 1:00 a.m.. An hour should be enough time for me to get to the spot, case it, then figure a way to get Edgar out without too much trouble." I said, laying the phone down.

There's some sub left on my torn wavy wrapper. Blood and juices from the spices have soaked through the wrapper I'm using as a place mat. I run a hand through the muck, mushing together what's left into a soggy bloody meatball. Red pinkish green liquid runs down my palm, my wrist, my forearm. Gladly I mash it all into my mouth, chewing, then licking myself of what's left on my fingers. I'm done. My head lowers to the table, awaiting sleep.

12 MOUNT VERNON

April and Kari sit quietly on the sofa in Kari's downtown apartment in Mt. Vernon, watching stand-up comedians on TV. Insert chapter ten text here. Insert chapter ten text here.

"I thought this would ease some of our pain but it hasn't." April said, blowing air from her pouting lips onto Kari's shoulder.

"Yeah, this is bullshit. Plus these fools ain't even funny!" Kari said, jumping up from the sofa, running into her bedroom.

April, a little startled, raises up to see what's going on.

"Kari what's wrong!?"

Kari doesn't answer.

April, fully gets up off the sofa and races to the bedroom herself. Simultaneously, Kari is leaving the bedroom. Destined to collide, Kari moves out of the way in time, having April whiz by into the bed.

"Damn girl, If I'd know you were that hard up for a drink, I would've had you come get this shit yourself." Kari said, laughing with an unopened bottle of vodka in her hand.

"Vodka? You jumped the hell off the sofa and ran in here to get some vodka!" screams April.

Kari laughs harder, going into the kitchen for two glasses. Unscrewing the top to pour, she nonchalantly moves out of the way of a pillow thrown at her by April.

"You still ticked at them comedians I see." Kari shouts, pouring the vodka.

"That was meant for you, huzzy."

"Girl. Come get this hooch before I drink your glass too."

April saunters into the kitchen looking Kari up and down then in a slow, playful nature takes the glass.

"To our men. May God comfort them and protect us all from evil."

Kari shouts.

"And shit that howl in the night too."

"Yeah girl. That too!"

Both take big swigs of the vodka then head back to the sofa.

"April, you are gonna pick that up, right?" Kari said, looking at the pillow on the floor.

April huffs, puts down her drink to pick up the pillow. She then sits with the pillow in her lap. Kari takes a another swig of vodka and lays her head in April's lap.

"Can we change the channel?" April asked.

On the floor is the remote, a few inches from the sofa on the floor between April's legs. Kari reaches down to pick up the remote, briefly touching April's calf. April exhales a bit, looking down at Kari who changes the channel to cartoons.

"Yeah. That'll work. Kari, how you gonna drink your drink with your head on my lap?"

"Magic." Kari said, producing a straw from her bra.

Both ladies laugh, drink and watch cartoons. Anything to ease the unimaginable horrors they've faced.

13 ROOSTER

Loud, annoying hollow 'rooster' sound screeches.

"Shit, I should've previewed that alarm." I grumble, fumbling to turn it off.

It's 11:45 p.m., it went off at the right time. I get up, pocketing my new cell to head to the front of Cray Cray's. Tami, Linda, Leroy, the tall keno drunk and one customer are present.

"You lucky we ain't want the place all fucked up from 5-O kicking your ass." Linda said.

Laughing, I blow a kiss at her and Tami then give a 'raised fist' to Leroy as I exit out of the Cray-Cray's.

Street lights pinch my eyes into a squint through the brisk heavy night air. I can make out people milling around Greenmount Avenue. Others are going into the liquor store, more than likely getting half pints or shorties of liquor to sneak into Shelby's, which has a line of party-goers wrapped around the corner. Barclay Street is two blocks away from where I am now. The the house where the dogfight is being held, is much further down, South towards 25th Street. Cray Cray's front entrance's angle enables me to avoid the crowd of faces going into Shelby's and the liquor store.

I ease away from Greenmount to the dogfight. Within 5 minutes, I encounter winos, potheads and other drug induced zombies, all oblivious to me, except one. To him, I'm his shadow. For a few seconds, he tries to make his body movements match mine. Increasing my pace throws him off, right into a parked car and onto the hard ass sidewalk. Stupid fuck is now cussing out his own shadow.

I needed that laugh since I'm only a block away from the dogfight house. Stupidity can sometimes ground you.

In front of me I see a few people get out of their cars walking South to the house. I stay a few yards away from the group to see which house they're going into when I see they're all going into 3719. It's 12:17 p.m.. I'm sending a text to Derek, letting him know it's about to go down.

The houses here are connected, two at a time separated by a ramshackle yard. The dogfight house is boarded up but not as much as the one next to it, 3721. Two large guys in long black coats are at the front of 3719. Two more near the rear. House 3723 is empty too. Its back yard is littered with 10 huge packing crates. They'll be good for me to use for cover.

Easily, I slip my way through the packing crate graveyard into an opening in the basement wall of house 3723. The darkness inside the basement is much darker than outside. Not having a flashlight and it being too risky to use the light from my new cell phone, I wing it. Going through the opening in the basement, I smell cigarettes, cheap cologne, dog shit, mold, rats and way too much perfume. These smells aren't overpowering like the earlier ones I had. Almost feels natural.

My new sense of smell guides my way in this empty dungeon of a basement up a worn down splintered stairway. Climbing carefully and quietly as possible, I make it onto the landing that leads into the kitchen. Lowering myself closer to the ground, someone flashes a light through the fragmented walls of what used to separate house 3721 and house 3723, just missing me. The light shines through the kitchen, dining room and upstairs area. I crouch behind a stove, putting me in the company of roaches, rats and other crawling shit.

Blowing my breath hard on them scatters them away from me. Whoever was flashing the light is satisfied that 'all is clear over here' and they leave, but my new crawling friends are coming back.

Standing up, I kick at the nasty little shits making them mad. A nearby wall opening helps me escape them. I step easily onto this floorboard with my prosthetic and can tell right away this part of the house is more sturdy. This leg is more sophisticated, the socket makes my stumps more sensitive to the contours of the ground I'm walking on.

When that person flashed their light earlier, I saw stairs to the left of one fragment of wall. Getting higher will give me a better vantage point. I just hope the stairs are as sturdy and sound as the floor. The first few steps up, there's little creaking, the rest of the steps, no creaking at all. Lucky me. I have a new problem now, suppressing my coughing. The crappy smells from earlier seem to be getting stronger.

Making it to the second floor without r coughing, I see what may have been a bedroom to my immediate right. It's tattered wallpaper, collapsing ceiling and broken furniture remind me of old crappy horror movies, especially with the way the moonlight slivers fight the forever floating dust particles and spider webs. Part of the floor is missing in this room, a good spot to see the sights below.

Before getting on my belly to slither to the edge of the hole, I check for rats and roaches, then my stuff. No creepy crawly shit around. New cell phone's on vibrate, wanted poster of Edgar and Hassan's amulet are in my pocket. Weapons ready.

On my belly, I squiggle to the edge to look over. Below, I see 12 men dressed in long grey t-shirts and khaki pants. They all have wads of money in one hand and a gun in the other. The areas wall are surrounded with what looks like padding of foam rubber. I guess to muffle the sound.

Along with these 12 men are 20 to 30 men and women, of many diversities, vying for their bids on the fights. Fifteen dogs, Pit Bulls, Shepherds, Rottweilers and Bulldogs, are corralled to the side of a makeshift pit, dug out of the dirt basement floor. Behind the dogs sits a plump ass guy in a director's style chair, I think is Edgar. He's wearing a bright orange hoodie that glows in the poorly lit arena. A long grey t-shirt guys runs over to him, giving him all the money that the other long grey t-shirt guys had. The guy I believe is Edgar, stuffs the money in his black cargo pants. The picture on my wanted poster has his ass clean-shaven with no distinguishing marks. This guy sports a full beard and a black eye patch over his right eye.

His movements around in the chair display a big fucking 'Edgar' belt buckle. Good enough declaration for my ass. He points to one of his long grey t-shirt guys who in turn yells,

"Alright, people. We starting this shit now. Y'all bets been made. Let's do this!"

Directly after the yelling, two dogs are released into the pit, an ivory pit bull, and a German Shepherd. The Shepherd draws first blood. Fangs engorge the neck of the Ivory Pit Bull followed by savage ripping bites to its left front shoulder. Blood oozing onto the ivory pit bull, colors its torso a dull magenta hue. The fierce fighting, intense violence, flying blood and savage sounds gives me a strange warm feeling inside. Almost like the feeling I get when having sex. The Ivory Pit Bull lunges at the front striking paw of the Shepherd, missing, yet clutches something better, the Shepherd's neck. Game over.

Low cheers and hushed jeers taint the sinful air. More money is collected and given to Edgar. Minutes later, two more dogs are guided into the pit. A large Black Rottweiler and another Pit Bull, this one Sunset Tan. Rearranging myself to get more comfortable, wood crackles beneath me. Looking below to see if I'm heard, no one looks up in my direction. The dogs barking and the din of the crowd drown out my sound. I move again, this time backwards. The wood cracks again. Holding my breath and tensing up my body I hear the long grey t-shirt announcer sound off again.

"Here's the next fight good people! Go!"

The dogs are released. Wood beneath me succumbs to my weight, having me crash to the first floor in a haze of rotted wood, molded plaster and decaying wallpaper..

"What the fuck was that!" Edgar yells.

I hear feet scrambling in my direction along with the dogs growls, snarls and that sharp clapping sound their jaws make as they snap at each other. I lay there quiet and still. Unseen, because of all the shit covering me. Beneath my body, I feel movement. The people I landed on are moving, so I thought. Bites follow, quick, sharp and many. Shit! I've landed on a rats nest.

My chest, neck, arms and leg are being inundated with a million stinging bites. I can't get up off of them because of the position I'm in and the weight of the crap on my back. My mental visual of being eaten alive by rats is more than I can bare.

My scream is muffled by the fat, vulgar, hairy bodies of the biting rats. My right stump, twitches, warming fast.

"Yo! There's somebody down here!" one of the long grey t-shirt guys yells.

That guy should have stayed by the dogs. Cocamoe is no longer Cocamoe.

Debris flies off of the werewolf like a running demon, exposed to holy water. Terrified rats charge everyone. Shock arrests all movements of the long grey t-shirt guy. His expungement, a chestful of werewolf claw.

All, including the dogs, look for an exit, any exit, from the surprise party from hell. The werewolf, snaps violently at people running hysterically by it when it leaps onto three of the long grey t-shirt guys, emancipating them from the living. Another long grey t-shirt guy shoots at the werewolf while running to protect Edgar. His bullets strike it, along with his three friends being shredded to death. Bullets have no effect on it at all.

"Shoot that fucker again!" Edgar screams, desperately looking for an exit that isn't blocked by dogs or humans.

Edgar's flunky, empties his gun into the werewolf feverishly thrashing its teeth into the three bodies. Annoyed, the beast lifts it's fiery eyes to focus on Edgar and the shooter. With it's snarls resembling a macabre smile, the monster springs forward, only to be stopped by a large black figure barreling into its chest. The werewolf topples hard and fast to the floor. The assailant, the Black Rottweiler.

"Yeah Sodom. Kill that fucker!" Edgar confidently yells.

That praise is promptly deflated when Sodom crashes brutally into the ground from being thrown directly at Edgar. Sodom's yelps, a strained drowning gurgle, are caused by a large chunk of its neck missing. The shattered dog hobbles away from the onslaught as the werewolf stands on its hind legs, eyeing Edgar and his long grey t-shirt guy. Blood, drips from its elongated snout as it slowly glances at the red pulsating gash in its upper left chest. Sodom's calling card.

The werewolf inches closer to Edgar. The long grey t-shirt guy wets his pants and begins to cry, pissing Edgar off. Chaos reigns devilishly throughout this house. The werewolf slashes its claws through those trying to get out as Edgar tries to think of his next move. With his head and mind swiveling around for direction, Edgar sees a path. Beneath his fallen chair is a grenade launcher.

"I've always wanted to use this shit for something." Edgar said, picking up and firing the weapon.

Hurtling in the direction of Edgar and pissy boy is the werewolf. It's flawless agility enables it to scathe past the scorching searing grenade. Behind behind the beast, a wall explodes crushing all trying to escape and the long black coat guys trying to get in. The werewolf berths two feet beyond Edgar and the wet one, it's position perfect for any carnage to be harvested.

Scythe-like efficiency from its claws dismount both heads. It's teeth lock down into Edgar's back to feed. The last long grey t-shirt guy with the wet pants is motionless, headless and upright. When his dead body's nerves jump start him into jerking dance-like movements. The werewolf momentarily withdraws from Edgar's divided back to watch. Soon the dead body's charge expires and it falls limp to the ground. It resumes its Edgar entree. The newly dead body will be its welcome dessert. Needless to say, the police will not be getting any calls about this incident.

14 CONNECTIONS

Detective Norris stares at the pinboard in his office. It's adorned with pieces of paper, pictures, map diagrams, red stick pins and black string connecting the pins. Several of the pieces of paper have the name 'Joseph Cocamoe' emblazoned on them.

"There is a damned connection, but what?"

Biting his pencil for the thousandth time, his face draws a blank.

"Working late ain't you? What'd ya do, lose your house keys again?" Detective Brunson said, walking by Norris's office.

Detective Norris looks at his watch, 3:27a.m. Grimacing, he flips Detective Brunson the bird.

"Yeah, you wish." Brunson said, sashaying away, laughing.

Norris dismisses his comment. Too busy going over evidence in his notepad, again:

1. Tuesday night past - elderly couple massacred in their car in Seawell State Park

2. Wednesday morn next day - I get a call from citizen informing me that a Joseph Cocamoe, one of the city's fugitive recovery agents/bounty hunter, was robbed of wallet, clothes and prosthetic leg, at the same park. I go to site, Cocamoe is found a couple hundred yards from elderly massacred couples car, he has no idea how he got there or why he's even there, no idea who robbed him, further questioning leads nowhere.

3. Thursday night Club 898 - an animal, wolf-like thing, attacks and kills 28 people, one of whom is my cousin Shaun Farrior. In morning, lab said some blood at Seawell State Park crime scene matches that of Cocamoe, also water samples nearby have his DNA present. Informed Shaun, he seemed surprised, wolf hair strands found in car at Seawell State Park and Club 898. After killings, Joseph Cocamoe found naked, legless and unconscious in alley/rear of club. EMT takes him to Trinity Hospital, I

follow but can't question him because he's sedated. Detective Laboo from Central City at club scene and hospital.

4. Early Friday morning Trinity Hospital - Joseph Cocamoe, now suspect, being guarded at hospital by Officer Hardy. Suspect subdues Officer Hardy and escapes. Whereabouts unknown. Side Note* - suspect has girlfriend, Nurse Practitioner at Northeast hospital named April

Johnson. She and her friend Kari Butler, waitress at Lloyd's, are both under surveillance.

Norris flipping his pad closed, flops into his uncomfortable, ripped black leather chair. Positioning his ass for that elusive comfort spot that's never found, he takes a sip of the cold coffee that's been on his desk for two days. He gargles, spits, then sips again, this time swallowing. Norris picks up his small tape recorder, pressing record he speaks into the microphone;

"October 4th, early Sunday morning, 3:40 a.m.. This is Detective Jerry Norris. Major Brown, The Commissioner and Mayor Warrington are coming down hard on me on this one. Body count this week at 30. Media coverage high and not so flattering. We still have vague leads, talk in town is 'there's a werewolf in Baltimore', I'm not sure if the Seawell State Park murders are connected to Club 898 murders. Werewolf, real funny. Maybe they're a new gang or something."

Detective Norris pushes the 'stop' button, gets up to leave to go home for the night.

15 CHARLES VILLAGE

Werewolf's done feeding. Looking around the abandoned house, there's nothing living left to eat. Thirst and rest are needed. It eases out of 3719 into the backyard, trotting away. Currently the streets are quieter, darker and outcast, no more edible souls. The werewolf's trot has it travel into an area of Baltimore named Charles Village. A quaint neighborhood with a mixture of bohemians, hippies, good juju, bad juju and college students. Beyond the beast is a small lawn being watered by an electronic sprinkler. Stopping to drink from an already formed puddle includes a cleaning. Humanity blood's and evil wash off the horrid matted fur mixing into the soil, shocking and confusing the thirsty green foliage. A few more laps of water are slurped by its coarse bitter tongue. It's not comfortable with its surroundings, there's no cover for rest so it leaves. It's destination, unknown. Part of the city sleeps, others continue to bleed.

16 HASSAN'S DAMNED HORSE

Hassan's horse neighs and brays loudly, kicking the stall walls violently. One by one, neighborhood lights flick on this early Sunday morning. People are yelling and cussing out of their windows, awakened by his horse.

"It's 5:49 in the damned morning Arraber! Quiet that stupid ass horse!" a neighbor yells.

Awaken, Hassan limping as fast as he can to his horse trips on something in the grass next to the stall. It's Cocamoe, naked, legless and unconscious. He has to get Cocamoe inside but his horse needs him first. Hassan goes to the stable chanting softly an African song, stroking his horse's mane to calm him. Angry shouts continue, even after the horse has settled down.

Hassan has now gotten Cocamoe up over his strong shoulders, carrying him into the house. He places Cocamoe in the pale room, covering him with a blanket then goes to check again on his horse. Slowly the neighborhood, Hassan and his horse have gone back to sleep. Tranquility, for now.

My right eye barely opens. The left opens fully. Collecting my surroundings, I can make out the pale room. Brown orange thin-assed blanket on my body, pomegranate incense and cannabis is smelled. I'm in Hassan's house, but how?

Sitting up, the blanket falls off my upper body.

"Shit! I'm naked again!"

Underneath the blanket, at my waist, I see I'm legless too.

"Fuck, not again!"

Hassan limps fast into the pale room.

"You're up. Good. It's way past two in the afternoon."

"Look old man. I don't care about that. How'd I get here like this and what did you do to my front shoulder. It's sore as shit?"

"Found you by the stall this morning, carried you in. I never touched your shoulder. So, you have no idea how you got here with your nakedness and legless too."

"No I fucking don't!"

"You remember nothing, nothing at all?"

"What are you, deaf! No I don't!"

"Don't get angry with me. I've done nothing to you."

"Sure you haven't."

"You to remember, anything. Anything at all."

I'm too annoyed to think, then a name pops into my head.

"Edgar!"

"Who?"

"Edgar, Edgar Quali. I went to collect him last night....dogfight on Barclay. I vaguely remember anything then I wake up here."

"Interesting."

"What the hell you mean by that old man?"

"Nothing, I just find that interesting, that's all."

"So, old wise one. You have any mystical reason for any of this shit?"

"Only mystical thing is your new connection to me and my house, otherwise, you just became one with the beast again."

"Whatever. I thought your stupid amulet was to stop 'me being the beast'."

"It's not stupid, and you're right, it should've. Where is it?"

"Where's what?"

"The amulet."

"Well...it ain't up my ass. That's for sure!"

"Interesting."

"Will you can that 'interesting' shit. For a motherfucker who knows all, you don't know shit. You know any damned clothes I can put on!"

"Watch your language. I have clothes but no leg for you."

"Got one in Andrew's car, front seat."

Hassan leaves to get these clothes he mentioned.

"Hey old man, why ain't your horse bugging out right now?" I shout.

"He was given a potent tea. He'll be out for a few days. I need him sedated while you're here. I'll lose some money but I'll save a life." he shouts back.

"Isn't that sweet. Hurry up old man with those clothes!"

I try to remember how I got to Hassan's house naked, with no leg. Hard to retrace my steps when there are none to follow. My left front shoulder isn't sore any longer, pain completely gone. How'd I get this new closed wound anyway. Hassan breaks my train of thought by coming in with the clothes.

"This will fit you."

Hassan hands me this green, red, ivory piece of fabric. Unfolding it, I feel the cool, soft, gentle touch of a long dashiki. As it unrolls onto the floor the linen interwoven silk aroma fills the room. Grinning, I cut my eye to Hassan.

"It's long enough to fit your tallness. It belonged to a Watusi Warrior Chief."

"Ok. Thanks. I think."

"Cocamoe. Give me the key to that car you have covered up so I can get your leg."

My look to Hassan says, "you dumb ass."

"Oh. Yeah, found you naked." Hassan said.

"It's not locked anyway. Just lift up the cover a little bit"

Hassan limps out, laughing.

I place the dashiki over my head, feeling how great it feels against my skin. Soft, cool and loose. Rippling caressing chills wave down my upper body, relaxing me. Haven't felt this way in a long long time. My need to decompress gets hammered by the fact that I remember close to nothing about last night.

Ill-timed, again, Hassan comes back into the pale room making me lose any train of thought that may have been coming. He hands me my prosthetic. It's old and crappy with an antiquated connection to my upper leg being straps, a belt wraps around my thigh and a thick ace bandage type covering over my knee so this shit won't fall off. My newer ones are connected with a long neoprene covering that's connected to the prosthetic then to my thigh, providing suction for extra support.

Placing it upon my stump, the strap doesn't fit that well. I've gained weight since I had this one fitted and inside the actual prosthetic stem there's a stupid ass screw loose. But once it's connected to my thigh, I make some adjustments for comfort and support. Hassan helps me to my feet.

"Before you leave, there are some conventional clothes in that bag in the corner that'll fit you too."

"Conventional clothes? Old crazy fuck….Why didn't you give me those first?"

"The dashiki covered your stuff quicker."

"Glad you find humor in my fucked-up-ness old man!"

"No. Nothing funny about what you are. I gave you that dashiki to quell your mind. Conventional clothes for you to put on when you go out and find Wepwawet." Hassan said, sternly and forcibly.

"Go out where?"

"Where you were last night."

"I don't know where I was last night old man!"

"Edgar." Hassan said.

"Oh. Edgar."

Limping away from Hassan, my stump is nearly conforming to the unnatural fit of the prosthetic socket. My limp-walk gets me to the furthest part of the pale room as I think and try to remember anything, anything besides the name 'Edgar'.

Frustration almost overcomes me when an internal flash whizzes through my head.

"3719 Barclay! Barclay and blood!"

Now limping excitedly back towards Hassan, stump was almost fully set within prosthetic socket.

"3719 Barclay and blood? Well that's where you're going, but after you eat. That blood memory is probably dogs mangling one another. I pray that's what it means." Hassan said, looking at me strangely going in the direction of the kitchen.

Following Hassan, I wonder about his tone when I said 'blood'. That wonderment goes away when I see Hassan cracking four eggs, sprinkling them with herbs and spices into a frying pan on the hot plate. In a smaller pan on another hot plate he throws in several slices of plantains, ginger and lemons. Mashing the plantains, mixing in the ginger and lemons heavily.

"No meat?"

"You've had more than enough."

Confused at his statement, I sit pulling the stool from under the table. Food smells great. Hassan brings over a wooden pitcher of tea, pouring us both a glass. He prays, makes a toasting gesture to which I comply, then we eat.

"Slow down. Food is dead. Not moving." Hassan said, as I inundate my mouth with food and drink.

I slow down, but not by much. Hassan notices my fondness for the tea and pours my fifth glass.

"Dried plantains, a few dried bananas, watermelon juice, some ginger and raspberry. My tea, you like, I see."

"Yes. Not bad." I said, feeling a bit strange. I just woke up, but now feeling extremely sleepy.

Hassan is chipper, ambling around the kitchen, clearing the table. For some reason the kitchen is getting darker. I'm saying something to him but I can't understand what I'm trying to say. My speech is slurred. Why? Hassan walks behind me and I attempt to turn my body in his direction but darkness cradles me.

17 THE PALE ROOM

Cocamoe falls into Hassan's arms and is carried into the pale room, laid down and covered with the brown orange blanket.

"He'll be out for a couple of days. Now I can create a mixture to remedy you from being one with the beast since my amulet is gone." Hassan said.

Cocamoe was given the same tea Hassan gave his horse for sedation. Hassan also drank the same tea, ages of training makes him immune to its power. Going into the room where he himself sleeps, Hassan goes to a wall, removing a large painting of the God Ra rising over the Nile river. Uncovered is a safe encased into the wall. Hassan presses a few numbers on a panel next to the safe door until a soft 'click' is heard. A pleasant intoxicating aroma strokes Hassan's nose, cheeks, neck and spirit, after the heavy steel door is opened. His safe protects small linen pouches holding spices, herbs, small glass vials with fragrances of African oils, small statues of Egyptian, Sudanese, Libyan and Chad deities along with rolled papyrus tied with cannabis string. There's also a book covered with worn slightly tattered dark brown leather binding. Hassan removes all of the linen spice bags, three vials of oil and two reams of the rolled papyrus documents. Items are placed onto the floor next to a gourd filled with water. He kneels in front of these items, says a prayer, then unrolls one of the reams, reading aloud the writing on the papyrus.

"What I do, I need the gods to give me the strength, wisdom and courage to obtain resolution. Mighty Wepwawet lead me, guide me, protect me and the soul of the one with the beast."

After these prophetic words, Hassan unties all the spice bags, mixes them with the three oils into the gourd using a small thick heavy stick then reads the other ream of papyrus, but to himself. This ritual, lasts 3 hours. The proper consistency of mixture is known to Hassan when the items coagulate into a deep dark black liquid with splashes of red streaks.

It's smell of spoiled fruit left in the sun is another indication of its readiness.

Hassan unwinds his erstwhile body from the kneeling position he's held for so long. Laying on his back, he extends his legs and arms upward towards the ceiling. Gently turning his body to the right, He gets on his hands and knees, slowly raising up to stand. Stretching fully, Hassan goes to the pale room, checking on the sleeping Cocamoe. Satisfied, Hassan goes into his kitchen to drink a bowl of mango juice. There he views the sun rays barging through the loose rafters of the stable. He bows to the sun, finishes his mango juice and leaves the kitchen to go back into his room to rest. Before settling down, he removes an empty gourd from behind a peacock statue, pouring in that mixture he created for Cocamoe. Corking the gourd, Hassan says another prayer then settles down to sleep.

18 SEEKING

"You ready?" April asks, placing a crucifix in her purse.

"Ahhh...What's that for? It's a werewolf not a vampire."

"Werewolves don't exist, neither do vampires. You saw what I saw. So whatever that thing is the good lord will stop it."

"Ok, whatever. You know they're going to try and follow us." Kari said, looking cautiously out the vertical blinds at obvious police cars, although unmarked.

"That's why we're taking two cars. We'll lose them in rush hour traffic, then meet at the Reptile House at the Zoo. It's 7:00 a.m. now, we'll meet at 10:00AM. That should be enough time to ditch them." April said.

"Yeah, ok."

"If you can't lose them, improvise."

Without hesitation, they head out, going to their own cars. April drives East, Kari drives West, with two of Baltimore's finest following each. The officers report in to Detective Norris that both women are leaving the house in separate cars and what direction they're going. Norris is out of bounds and jurisdiction in having two of his men monitor and tail the ladies. For some reason Central City HQ isn't too concerned about April and Kari.

Detective Norris was already in his car driving down the Alameda, and is stopped at a red light on 33rd Street. To his right, the majestic tower of his Alma Mater.

"City forever!", Norris whispers, while picking up his car radio microphone for an update from his two officers.

"Car 1203, what's your location?"

"President St. and Albemarle."

"Car 119, what's your location?"

"Edmondson and Rolling Road."

"Stay in pursuit."

Norris makes a left turn onto St. Paul Street, looking for Cocamoe too, but he has to make a stop by Club 898 then on to Seawell State Park.

Concurrently, Detective Laboo is trudging to his car in East Baltimore. He's also looking for Cocamoe as he starts dialing Detective Norris's cell phone. The first few numbers are pressed then he stops.

"I need to find this Cocamoe asshole fast and get to the bottom of the Club 898 murders." Laboo said, walking to his car.

In West Baltimore the unmarked Blue Chevy Malibu follows Kari's car. Her nerves, beyond agitation as she checks the time on her dashboard, 9:05 AM. A red traffic light stops her at the intersection of Frederick Road and the I 695 on ramp. Driving around West Baltimore for two hours to shake this cop is wearing on her. She's tried, but not hard enough. The Blue Chevy Malibu is three cars behind her at the red light. In an instant, Kari steps on the gas pedal, barely missing the car in front of her as she makes a hard left U-turn into traffic. Oncoming cars screech to dramatic stops, making split second avoidance maneuvers from hitting one another and Kari. This tactic creates a major tie-up, trapping the Blue Chevy Malibu in a horn blowing metal labyrinth.

Kari doesn't bother looking back, her attention is focused on not killing herself.

"Sir! Car 119. I just lost her."

"What!"

"Sir, she did this crazy move with her car by the I 695 on ramp causing a huge pile up and I couldn't pursue."

"Come on car 119! When you lost her, which direction was she headed?"

"East on Frederick Avenue, driving a white Toyota Camry with vanity tags 'EATME'."

"Eat me?"

"Yes sir, Elephant Apple Tango Minnesota Elephant."

Kari, 3 miles away from where she made her getaway, makes a left turn onto Rock Glen Road, speeding up it's hill. At the top of the hill there's a gas station where she sees a cab pulling in. Slowly herself down, Kari gets an idea.

"Excuse me sir. Sir, excuse me. My car is breaking down and it's about to stop. I have an important meeting to get to. May I hire you?" Kari said, sweetly as she pulls up next to the cab.

The cabbie looks at her car, then Kari herself. She's sure the police has everyone looking for her car by now and she hopes this new other crazy tactic works too.

"I'm getting coffee, then I'm all yours." said the cabbie.

"Oh great. My treat then sweetie." Kari said, getting out of car.

After a few minutes they are both back at the cab with the cabbie's coffee.

"Where to ma'am?"

"Celtic Park Reptile House."

Meanwhile, in the aftermath of car's 119 ordeal, Detective Norris reaches out to car 1203.

"Car 1203, your location!"

"Martin Luther King Boulevard and Washington Boulevard."

"Do not lose her!"

"Don't worry, I've got her. "

April's mindset is on the amount of traffic, the traffic lights and the Brown Chevy following her Black Lexus. Her dashboard clock reads 9:35 AM. Traffic ahead of her slows, pulling over.

"What the hell is going on!" April shouts.

Behind her is an ambulance, lights flashing with no siren blaring. A block in front of the slowing traffic ahead of April is a funeral procession. They're slowing for the ambulance too. April can now see the funeral procession further up and she lets the ambulance pass, then accelerates directly behind it. The Brown Chevy speeds up too.

April's approximately three feet behind the fast-moving ambulance before it slows to make a right turn onto Fayette Street forcing April to swerve left to not hit the ambulance. She's traveling fast, straight into the funeral procession of cars, still slowing and pulling over for the ambulance. A space between the moving hearse and family limousine opens. April seeing it, zooms through. The Brown Chevy gains on April, unfortunate for the officer, the hearse slows down considerably after April's car whizzes by. The officer is going too fast to compensate for any maneuvering and he crashes into the heavy hearse. Glass, metal, and flowers scatter throughout onto Martin Luther King Jr. Boulevard. The officer in car 1203 smashes his dashboard several times in anger before he picks up his car radio microphone.

"Detective Norris. I lost her sir. I had a car accident."

"Accident, c'mon now! Y'all can't follow a damned waitress and a nurse. Shit! What's make, model, the color of car and direction. Also, did you happen to get a license plate before your accident?"

"North on MLK, Black Lexus LS500, vanity tag 'ERN' Edward Robert Nancy."

Dismayed, Detective Norris doesn't call in an APB for fear of departmental repercussions.

The hearse driver views the damage to his hearse and coffin as he approaches the officer's car to check on him. Other funeral home staff members rush to check on the grieving family and the hearse driver. All parties try to maintain order as they attempt to piece together what just happened.

During this time, Kari's cab is a block from the Zoo entrance. April herself, is already there, parked on the side of the Reptile House, waiting.

The time on her clock reads 9:58 a.m. when she sees a taxi pull up behind her car. Already apprehensive, anxious and nervous, she feels better when she sees Kari getting out of the taxi.

"Where's your car and who's that?" April asked.

"Had to ditch it, they were on me tight. Cabbie is my new friend. I asked him if he'd help us look for Cocamoe by driving us around. 5-O probably looking for your car too, so you may want to leave it here. Cabbie's already agreed to help."

"Really?" April said, very suspiciously.

"Yeah, really." Kari said, pouting.

April agrees. Gets out of her car, locks it and walks to the taxi with Kari.

"Do we have to pay him?" April asked.

"Nope."

April stops in her tracks pulling Kari's arm to stop her too.

"Do we have to screw him? I'm not screwing him!"

"Woman calm down, no screwing, pulling or sucking. I explained our issue and he was pleased to help."

"Our issue?"

"Yeah. My brother has Alzheimer's and we need to find him before the police do because of the money and Social Security issue. He said he fully understands avoiding 'the man'."

April smiles shakes her head at Kari.

"We'd better find 'our brother' girl."

Getting to the cab, Kari introduces the two.

"Omar. This is my girlfriend April. April this is Omar."

"Nice to meet you, ma'am. Remember, no fuckey no suckey." Omar said, smiling.

"Ow!" Kari shouts, from being punched in the arm by April.

"Where to ladies?"

"Pimlico," April said.

Omar heads off in the direction of Pimlico, the famed race track area of Baltimore.

In the drive there, both women look for Cocamoe's face on the faces of men plodding around on Baltimore's streets.

"Why are we going to Pimlico?" Kari asked.

"It's one of Cocamoe's hang out spots. He used to bounce at a reggae club in the area and friends up here stay loyal to him."

"Oh. Okay."

"Hey, nice lady. What does your brother look like again?" Omar asked.

Both ladies look at one another for a quick second, slightly puzzled because neither of them has a brother.

"Six-three, fine Black man with short hair, sexy face, cut body and walks with a limp. May look confused." Kari said, quickly. Transforming her voice into a soothingly excited tone which gets a mean glare from April.

"Yeah. He looks real damned confused!" April shouts.

"That sounds like half the Brothers on my route."

Riding through the Pimlico neighborhood of dank alleys, vague side streets, obscure grand thoroughfares, and stops at the occasional stores, come up empty. April laughs when she had Omar stop at an 'occasional store'.

"Why do you call them 'occasional stores'?" Kari asked.

"Girl, Cocamoe calls them that. He said that even though they are supposed to be convenience stores, when you go in they 'occasionally' have what you need or looking for."

With this area giving an empty search, April asks Omar to ride down by Noir Marsh Mall, five miles South of the Pimlico area. If he's not found there she wants to ride to Cherry Hill. Perhaps they'll spot his truck or Cocamoe himself outside the mall or in Cherry Hill.

Driving to Noir Marsh Mall, Omar's taxi is constantly hailed by those on the street. Ignoring them receives a barrage of cussing, fussing, and fingers. Ignoring them all, he makes it to Noir Marsh Mall, pulling slowly into the parking lot with them all looking for Cocamoe.

This mall, one of Baltimore's transportation hubs, is where humanity greets, meets and sometime consummates before they 'get' to where they're going or 'stay' where they're going. Humans can catch the subway, a bus, a taxi or a hack, all designated to ferry people to hell or home.

No signs of Cocamoe there either.

"This is a no-go. Let's hit Cherry Hill. Please" Huffs April.

Omar wheels his taxi out of the parking lot, driving South on Pennsylvania Avenue. Kari and April take another check behind them for Cocamoe when Kari's cell rings. The number displayed is an unlisted one. It may be Cocamoe.

"Hello?" Kari said, a little unsettled about an unlisted number showing up on her phone.

"Hi, Kari. This is Jerry. Jerry Norris….Ummm, Detective Norris."

"Oh. Hi Jerry…..I mean Detective Norris."

April, hearing his name immediately looks behind her.

"I've been meaning to call you, to you know, say I'm sorry about Shaun. I wanted to say something to you at the hospital but everything was confusing and rushed", Kari said.

"Thank you. Really appreciate that. I'm sorry for your loss too. I know how much Shaun meant to you. Kari, I was wondering if you'd be able to help me with the finishing touches of Shaun's funeral arrangements. You know, the program. The funeral is Thursday, 3 PM?"

"Funeral arrangements, the program? Ahhh....Yeah, sure. I'd love to."

"You sure? This may be hard for you. I really wasn't sure if I should even ask but you and ...."

"Stop. I'll be ok."

"Great. This will help me out a lot. Can we meet at Lloyd's, tomorrow? Say around 7 PM?"

"Sure. Tomorrow, Lloyd's at 7."

"Cool. Thanks a lot. Hey Kari, one more thing. Where are you headed right now?"

Kari pulls the cell away from her head fast, looks at April then places cell back up to her ear.

"You know very well where I'm headed," Kari said, in a very sexy alluring tone.

There's momentary silence from all parties. The two ladies look behind them again for Norris or any police but none are seen. Then you hear Detective Norris laughing through the cell phone earpiece.

"Yeah, Kari. I know. Y'all be careful. If you find him, please call me."

"No problem. Will do Jerry. Bye Detective."

"Bye Kari."

Before Kari could disconnect the call, April starts rubbing two fingers together in a 'shame on you' fashion.

"What?"

"What's the deal with you and Jerry?".

"Go to hell smart ass. Don't have time for your pettiness woman. Later on, I'm going to help my man's cousin with funeral arrangements!"

"Ladies! Hey ladies! Is that your brother?"

Omar's stopped at a stop sign, letting this man cross the street. All are quiet, watching this large dark man with a heavy limp, go across. His head is turned away from the taxi until Omar blows his horn, startling the guy. The guy turns, facing the taxi, slamming his fist hard on the hood. His dark angry face with a large scar across the forehead and a left eye much larger than the right eye, scares the women.

"No. That ain't him!" they shout in unison.

Omar apologizes. The scowl on the man dissipates, noticing the women in the back seat.

"Go! Now! Go, drive Omar, drive!" April shouts.

The man grimaces again as he pounds the roof of the cab as it speeds away.

"Sorry ladies."

"Don't worry about it Omar. Just get us to Cherry Hill." April said, looking at the grinning Kari.

Cherry Hill, a close-knit African American waterfront community on the Patapsco River is April's home. Cocamoe grew up here too, then moved when he joined the Army. April's seldom a passenger when coming home, so she takes in Cherry Hills' beauty and wonderment. Omar's route takes them from Waterview Avenue, site of the popular seafood restaurant Blue Waters, to Cherry Hill Road, where the shopping center reigns.

Before getting to the shopping center at the top of the hill, they ride pass several small manufacturing businesses, a light-rail train stop, an indoor swimming pool, several apartment complexes, single family houses and churches. If Cocamoe is out here, he'd be in the shopping center or someone there may have seen him.

"Pull into the shopping center Omar." April said.

Faces stare longingly at the taxi, leery of it's slow movement, wary of its occupants. Several faces recognizing April wave, she returns the greeting.

"Flower, Hey Flower!" A voice familiar to April, shouts out her family nickname.

"Stop the taxi please." April said, looking for that friendly voice.

Coming up to the taxi is her God-father, Uncle Rip, a retired steelworker, getting his weekly lottery tickets from the liquor store. Her smile grows as she gets out to hug and kiss Uncle Rip.

"Hi, Unc. How've you been. My, my, you look good, ain't seen you in a while. Getting your lottery numbers in I see."

"Gotta play, to win. You're looking good too Flower. I'm good, family's all good. How've you been." Uncle Rip said, smiling broadly at his beautiful God-daughter.

"I'm good, real good. Me and my girl Kari are out here looking for Cocamoe. Hey Kari, this is my God-father Rip Middleton. Unca Rip, this is Kari, and our driver Omar. Have you seen Cocamoe?" April said, between the waves of the three being introduced.

"Naw, ain't seen him in about a month or two. You know how he's always going to different parts of the country hunting people down."

"Somebody need to hunt your butt down!" Another voice rings out behind Uncle Rip.

April looks behind Uncle Rip and sees two more uncles, Rip's brothers, Freddie and Cardinal, walking up. She runs to them, giving them a tight group hug and kiss.

"C'mon girl, not too rough, ya might knock my teeth out." Uncle Cardinal said, laughing.

"Maybe that's what you need to shut you up." Uncle Freddie replies.

"Wow it's great seeing you all"

"Girl where's your car, why you in a cab?" Uncle Cardinal asks.

"My car's being serviced and me and my girl Kari here where doing some shopping and we were in the Hill so I came up here to see if I ran into Cocamoe."

Uncomfortable with the huge lie she's telling her family, April watches Kari and Omar looking around the shopping center for signs of Cocamoe. She really wants to get away before more family show up and more lies come out.

"No, we ain't seen him in a while. Why not call him?" Uncle Freddie said.

"I did. Keeps going to answering machine."

"Maybe he's igging you or he's on assignment." Uncle Cardinal said.

"Leave Flower alone. Cocamoe will turn up, don't worry. We're gonna get Cardinal home before somebody that he owes money to sees him." Uncle Rip said, laughing while placing a big kiss on April before hugging her.

"Ok. It's always great seeing you three. Me and Kari have to get more shopping in."

All four hug again, kiss, then part ways. No signs of Cocamoe there either.

19 POLICE TAPE

Outside Club 898, Detective Norris walks by torn police tape and three employees in front cleaning up some of the chaos that's left. Norris flashes his ID fast heading towards the rear bathroom, hoping Laboo or anyone from Central City Police District will show up.

Norris notices the remarkable difference of the insides of the club from last time he was there. Interior looks brand spanking new. The broken tables and chairs are gone, mirrors are replaced and the bars are being rebuilt. However, some remnants of death's visit remain. With the lights on, Norris views that all blood is not fully gone, walls and speakers are freckled with it.

One of the employees that was outside comes inside carrying a ladder, a small bucket, rubber gloves, a spray bottle and rags. His destination, the dried blood on the ceiling. Norris watches a bit, then heads to his own destination. Where the killings started.

Both bathroom stalls in the men's room, still depleted of bathroom stalls, is where Norris start his investigating. In a zen-like manner; eyes closed, mime-like hand gestures and body movements, Norris stops abruptly. He looks in the newly placed mirror, trying to fit Cocamoe into this awkward puzzle.

"Shit! Maybe Cocamoe is the animal. When he changes, he takes his leg off because it ain't natural to the animal." Norris said, almost in the neighborhood of grasping the imagery of the true butchery here.

Norris checks his watch, 5:27 p.m. He's done getting his fill of hell for the day.

"I've been reading too many of those crazy books of Shaun's about the occult and werewolves. Time to go find Cocamoe and his two women."

20 BALTIMORE: THE EASTSIDE

On the East side of Baltimore, at the same time Norris's leaves Club 898, Detective Laboo is walking to his car near William Frances Middleton hospital. He's drinking the last of his coffee, following up on a lead on another case. He feels and hears his hunger pangs calling him, along with someone in the background.

"Got a light."

Detective Laboo looks behind him. It's a guy he's had run ins with before, LB, one of the East-side of B-more's street urchins.

"My man LB. What's up! How you been, how's it hanging!" Laboo said, as he turns around and bluntly escorts LB to the buildings wall, frisking him.

"Yo man what's the deal. I don't need this cruelty. I ain't got shit!" LB shouts.

Laboo finishes his frisking and releases LB's black satin jacket.

"Thank you!" LB shouts, straightening out his jacket from Laboo's wardrobe assault.

"You're welcome. Tell me what happened last week at Club 898."

"What's to tell that you don't already know."

"I want the hoods perspective."

"Whatever man."

"C'mon LB you know the routine. Start talking. I really don't want you in my car."

"I don't wanna be in your car, man. So just chill, straight up, a monster, big bad wolf type motherfucker ate a whole bunch of little pigs, not any police ones. You know, it's just a metaphor, you dig."

"Yeah I dig. You're about to dig my foot outta your ass. What's this shit about this big bad wolf, monster shit."

"Damn man, you don't know? The Supreme Being ain't happy with us humans so he sent one of his pets to clean house."

"You've been smoking that rock I see!"

"Naw man, I'm clean. Clean as a bone eaten by a wolf."

Laboo grabs LB by his jacket again, pressing lightly on his neck.

"Not the clothes impediment again. Don't get mad at me cause y'all can't catch the thing."

"I really don't know where you get this monster bullshit from. Rabid dog is what it is, big rabid dog."

"Ok, 'rabid dog' if that's what y'all call it downtown. Now you got your 'hood perspective'. Can I go? I'm trying to get inside before it gets dark." LB gurgles.

Laboo senses that LB is telling the truth and scared as shit for some odd reason, so he releases him.

"Straight up though. My Lil' brother was there at Club 898 that night, he's on the up n' up, you know college kid n' shit, flying right. He told me this thing in the club was a werewolf, live and in person. Also, heard some other crazy shit happn'd up on Barclay by 25th street, real nasty shit. Bodies still there. Been there for a couple days with dead pooches too. You n' your boys might wanna check up that way."

"Barclay, dead bodies, dead dogs, werewolf!" Laboo scoffs.

"Whatever man. You either care or don't, I don't give a shit. Man it's getting dark, I'm ghost." LB said.

"Go, get the fuck outta here. You're just damned crazy as shit!" Laboo said, checking to see if there's any damage done to his suit.

"Crazy but alive!" LB shouts, running up the street.

"Hey, what address on Barclay!" Laboo screams, brushing pieces of lint and dirt off his pants leg.

LB's out of earshot, desperate to beat the wickedness coming Baltimore's way.

"Shit. Somewhere on Barclay and 25th Street. I'll have a patrol car ride over and check it out." Laboo said, walking again to his car.

Three blocks have been walked when Laboo stops, he doesn't see his car.

"Where the hell is my car? Did I park this far up?"

Laboo turns around, walking back towards the hospital, thinking that little scruff he had with LB threw off his direction. In three feet of going the opposite direction, Laboo eyes his car in the alley. Huffing, he pats several of his pockets, looking for his car keys when he pats a pack of cigarettes and lighter in his front jacket breast pocket.

"I did have a light." Laboo smirks, also finding his keys in that pocket.

Laboo notices how empty the street are. Strange, especially since it's not that late out and the hospital surroundings always have people milling about. Unlocking the driver's side door Laboo hears something fall in the narrow alley behind him. He plays it off as he pulls the key out of the door, thinking it's probably a rat, cat or dog.

A second noise, low growls and heavy breathing, isn't ignored Using the driver side window as a mirror to see behind him, Laboo sees nothing but black. Growls and breathing grow louder. He turns around, hand on gun still in holster. The unseen visitor's breathing quickens.

Laboo's draws his weapon, pointing into the void. Heart's racing, trying hard to catch up with his breathing. His head's on a controlled frightened swivel has no visual contact, the darkness blackens even more. Ambient sounds are gone, they've been frightened away.

Not waiting to be see what the black unknown reveals, Laboo snaps open the car door getting inside fast, pulling it closed behind him faster. Instantaneously, a crashing forceful thud is felt against the car door. Laboo's body, designer suit and all, is thrown to the other side of the car, disengaging him from his gun. Something wants in.

Seconds later, a second jolt to the car slides Laboo headfirst under the passenger side dashboard. The parked car's being forced sideways by something big and unseen, forcing the tires to squeal like a pig going to slaughter. Then there's silence.

The jarring smell of burned rubber double-dutches on Laboo's senses. Disheveled and unnerved, he manages to pull himself from under the dashboard. Finding his gun, he crawls over to the driver's seat rising slowly to look slightly out the closed slightly cracked driver's side window, seeing nothing. The other windows are intact. There's still no visual of the intruder. Laboo quickly fumbles around his open glove compartment to get his flashlight. Once more, he sits up to his left, gaining some leverage to look over the car door without lowering the window. Peering out with the flashlight he finds only two thick black tire marks of where his car used to be.

"Assholes!" Laboo snarls, placing the flashlight in the passenger seat.

Doing a quick look again at his intact windows, Laboo starts the car, uncloaking the death shrouded silence. Before pulling off, he picks up the flashlight to take one more look out the driver's side window. There's something in the distance. A figure. A figure so dispiriting it seems to absorb all light into itself. Whatever it is, it's moving, getting larger and faster by the second.

Laboo lowers the window but that slight crack it has prevents it from going fully down. With the gun still in his left hand, he aims at the leaping figure which reaches its apex the same time the gun is fired. Glass explodes, intertwining into an enlightened impressionistic deluge of fangs, fur and unholiness. Thus, becoming the new light to the before mentioned darkness.

This creature's opened mouth encases Detective Laboo's gun and hand.

More bullets find freedom inside it as it falls heavy, hard and dead atop of Laboo, flattening him into the seats. The dead animal, a large Black Rottweiler, has it's mouth full of blood, holes and Laboo's upper forearm. With great effort, he's able to withdraw his upper forearm, then pull himself from under the creature's weight to get out of the car.

"Damn. That was some crazy ass shit. This might be the thing that attacked Club 989. Wow did I shoot that thing that much?" Laboo said, viewing the animal and the large chunk of its neck missing.

Laboo flinches, stinging sensations in his left arm erupt. Looking at his arm close up in the darkness, he can make out several small pricks along with three long scratches. Blood trickles down his wrist.

"Fuck, damned dog's teeth scratched me and fucked up a good ass suit. This shit's going to be hard to explain. Good thing I have proof." Laboo said, kicking the animal in its ass, making it move.

Spooked, Laboo jumps away from the dog and car.

"Bitch ass!" he shouts, emptying the rest of his bullets into the animal's side.

Almost convinced that it's dead, Laboo goes to his trunk getting a t-shirts to rip for use as a tourniquet and the carjack. Before wrapping his arm he pokes the dead animal with the carjack and gets no movement. A good sign but it may be faking. Wary, Laboo inserts another clip in his gun and reaches inside his car to call this incident in.

"Dispatch. This is Detective Laboo. I've been attacked by a large, possibly rabid dog at the William Francis Middleton Hospital. Animal is dead, I'd like the forensics team here ASAP."

"Detective Laboo are you injured?"

"A few scratches. I'm at the hospital so I'll have them take a look."

"What's your exact location Detective?"

"Corner of Milton and Ascension."

"They're in route."

21 HASSAN'S CRIB

The sweet balm of homemade applesauce, eggs and mango juice fills the air in Hassan's kitchen. He places the finished product in a bowl, says a prayer then eats. After a few bites, he goes with bowl in hand, to check on the sleeping Cocamoe in the pale room. Content that he's still asleep, Hassan leaves to check on his horse.

"In due time my friend. In due time." Hassan said, stroking and kissing the sleeping animal gently.

Content that his horse will be fine, Hassan goes back into the house. He goes into the kitchen for a piece of modern technology he does own. A small radio kept in the refrigerator used for weather reports. Today, it'll be used to monitor the news for anything regarding Cocamoe. Hassan waits, eats more applesauce listening.

"Baltimore City Police are still on the lookout for Joseph Cocamoe. The famed Bounty Hunter, is being sought for questioning about the gruesome killings at popular downtown nightclub Club 898. If anyone has any information, please call 311 or 410-555-STOP." the radio DJ said.

"They won't find ya my boy, not here anyway." Hassan said, scooping up the last of his meal.

22 KARI

Kari pushes herself to leave the Powder Break, a dingy, but pleasant, out of the way motel on Deany Way, in the Southeastern part of Baltimore. She and April laid low there. It's Tuesday morning and April has taken days off from her job. Kari doesn't have that luxury.

"After work, don't forget I'm meeting with Jerry."

"I didn't forget. You're going to work? How you getting there. Is Omar out there?" April mumbles from under the blanket.

"Yes, I'm going to work. I can't poop around all day like you and Omar ain't out there, I'm catching a cab then bus."

"I'm not going to poop around all damn day. I gotta get up and look for Cocamoe." April said, removing the blanket from her head.

"Why don't you wait and meet me at Lloyd's round 8:30 PM then we'll look together, with Omar."

"Ok. Sure. Be careful."

Kari heads out the door, taking in the sunlight heading up Deany Way to hail a cab. April checks her cell for texts from Cocamoe. None are there. She puts it back on the nightstand, burying her head deeper into the pillow for more sleep.

23 DETECTIVE NORRIS

Later that evening, Detective Norris sits at his cluttered desk, reading the newspaper.

"Three days of relative calm. I don't like this." Norris said.

"Three days of calm? What city are you talking about? There've been 17 shootings, 4 deaths and 21 assaults, you call that calm?" Detective Flakeoski said.

"Flake you know what I mean."

"Why are you here? Don't you have something to do?" Flakeoski said, looking at his watch, 7:35 PM.

"Is it that late? Wow, I've got to go. Thanks for the reminder." Norris said, fooling around with items on his desk.

"Leave Norris. Now!"

"Ok, ok. I'm gone." Norris said, picking up a few personal items from his top drawer to prepare to meet with Kari.

Inside his car heading to Kari for the short ride, Norris thinks about his departed cousin. Images of Shaun's severed arm on the nightclub's floor along with the other desecrated bodies gives him a chill. Smiling and happy faces of passersby bring him back to Earth.

"We're all sheep herded by the wolf in man's clothing." Norris whispers, pulling up to Lloyd's.

Norris collects his stuff getting out of the car. He greets a few people walking past before swinging open Lloyd's door, releasing today's smell of the day. Specials of the day change but not the smells. Burned, greasy and spicy are mainstay smells. Detective Norris walks in, side-eyeing the waif of the frying onions on the grill. Kari, waiting tables, casually waves at him and points to an empty table in the rear. Norris nods at her while going to that table, laying his folder and notebook down he eases into the seat.

After a few minutes Kari finishes up with her last table, thanking her customers and picking up her tip. Kari, smiling at Norris, walks over to his table.

"Before we get started, I'd like to congratulate you in ditching my guys yesterday." Norris said.

Kari blushes, then lights into Norris with a flurry of yells.

"Why in the hell were they following us anyway! Why aren't they looking for that thing from the club and leaving us and Cocamoe alone!"

"Calm down please. We don't need a scene. They were protecting you both. Look Kari, I'm here for one reason, your help."

Softening her tone and demeanor, Kari relaxes a bit.

"How can I help?"

"Well, most of the program is done. I want you to tell me what you want said about your feelings towards Shaun. We'll do this, then I'll run over to the 24 hour print copying shop."

"Gee, put a sista on the spot, will you."

"Kari, you were all he talked about. I'm sure you can think of something to write or say."

"Give me a piece of paper and something to write with."

Detective Norris slides his small notepad and pencil to her across the table. Kari stares at those items for a few minutes, then writes.

'Shaun. You're that polished apple given to a favorite teacher. Sweet. You're that last swig of water given to drink on a dry hot day. Thoughtful. You're that relaxing position I've finally achieved before falling asleep after minutes of trying. Comforting. You're the egg to my bacon. Perfect. I will miss your physical touch. Everything else is still here. My heart holds you, my brain holds you, my soul holds you. Spiritually we touch everyday. I have and will love you forever.'

Kari slides the notepad over to Norris. Reading what she wrote, Norris's facial expression tells her that he approves. He glares up at Kari then back at the notepad, slamming it on the table.

"Where is he!"

"Oh hell no! Who's causing a scene now!"

Norris jumps up out of his seat getting closer to Kari, his voice now a harsh whisper.

"Kari. I know you know where he is. I can arrest you for obstruction of justice and harboring a fugitive."

Kari rears away from Norris. Lloyd's customers take notice.

"I'm not obstructing shit. You and your ass buddies just can't find him. Hell, me and April been looking for him too for two days and nights." Kari whispers, harshly.

"Kari you know what he did at Club 898. Do you want that to happen again!"

Puzzled, Kari's body stiffens.

"What the fuck are you talking about? What who did? Cocamoe? You trying to tell me that thing, that animal, that wolf thing was Cocamoe?"

"Not entirely sure. Putting pieces together and everything points to him. Shaun was the one, I think, who really knew and Cocamoe killed him."

Kari gets quiet, looks Norris straight in his eyes then gets up to leave.

"I can't believe you said that shit. Something is wrong with you. I'm out."

"Kari stop and sit down or you will be arrested!" Detective Norris shouts.

Now all of Lloyd's is in an uproar. A few remaining people duck behind tables, some stay in the hallway by the bathroom while the employees get low behind the counter, in case gunfire breaks out. Kari stops, turns to face Norris and returns to her seat, not saying a word through her gritted teeth. Norris realizes yelling is not going to get them anywhere, so he lowers his voice and mode.

"I really do need your help. I need to talk to Cocamoe, just talk. Sorry about what I said, didn't really mean it that way. I can explain if you let me."

Kari softens her face and body a little.

"In my investigation, with a little help from Shaun, this is what I have. Last Monday there was a grisly murder of an elderly couple in Seawell State Park. That morning, Cocamoe was also at the park, found naked and legless with no recollection of how and why he got there. Same week, on Thursday at Club 898, you and the rest were there witnessing a large hairy animal attack and kill 28 people. In the aftermath of the what happened in the club, Cocamoe is found naked, bloody, legless and unconscious in the alley...."

"You found his leg and ripped clothing in the bathroom. He was fighting that thing off." Kari interrupts.

"Guess you got that info from Shaun."

"No, I have other friends on the force."

"Ok, anyway. Shaun was reading a lot of those crazy books on werewolves and the occult. He was informing me on Cocamoe's reactions to stuff, his feelings, you know crap like that. He told me about Cocamoe's ordering and eating of raw food while here."

"Yeah. That raw food thing did kinda weird me out." Kari said.

"According to Shaun, Cocamoe was eventually, slowly changing into a werewolf. Sounds crazy and medieval but it's all I've got so far. The zoo has all of their animals, wolves, bears, hyenas, lions, tigers, jaguars and panthers accounted for. Park Rangers at all Maryland State Parks informed us that there are no records, written, visual or folklore of a violent large animal, especially a wolf, in the state."

"You mean no one knows about this werewolf thing theory?" Kari said.

"As far as I know, me, Shaun and you. You do remember your tirade at Trinity ER. Detective Laboo at Central City District may have the same crazy speculation." Norris said.

"Can we talk to this Laboo?" Kari asked, unsure of anything Norris said.

"So. You believe me?"

"Not yet. I believe there's a werewolf thing out there, but it's not Cocamoe. He's just getting crazier that's all. Also have to think of my girl April's safety."

"Where is she? I'd like to talk to her too."

"Just stop it right there. I told you, she and I looked for Cocamoe and didn't find him."

"Do you think she suspects he's a werewolf?"

"Hell no!"

24 MAYBE

My prosthetic ain't on. Uptight and scared, I can't really focus my eyes. All I can make out is white.

"Did I die and go to heaven?"

Head throbs. Prying open my eyes with my fingers, they're focusing on where I am. It's the pale room in Hassan's house. To my left, I make out my hated old prosthetic on the floor next to me. My mouth's dry and sticky. I call out Hassan's name but nothing's coming out. I pick up my old prosthetic and bang it on the floor and get no response from Hassan.

After a few minutes pass and no Hassan, I manipulate some spit to ease my mouths dryness. That shit's really not helping. I was going to call out again until I see a small bowl on the floor filled with water. I wonder why I didn't smell this shit and is it for me to drink or wash up with? Wasn't sure. I choose to drink it.

"Hassan!" I yell, after swallowing a few gulps.

Still no answer.

Fine, he's not here. I pull my old prosthetic closer, wondering where in the hell is my good one. Undoing the straps to attach it to myself so I can get me some food, I catch myself staring at this old artificial leg. Great memories with this thing. Like the time I met this babe in Troy, Minnesota at this bougie-ass nightclub. Can't remember her's or the club's name, but I was standing at the bar when she came over to order a drink. She bumps into my right leg, apologizing. I didn't acknowledge her because I didn't feel it. She felt ignored so she bumps me again, harder. Excusing herself. I said to her 'no problem, didn't feel it'. Brazenly, she hits my leg hard with her purse with her purse bounding back harder hitting her. I asked her 'why are you assaulting me' when, again, she apologizes, then asked if I'm a war vet or something. I told her 'something'. She asked if I'm wearing a prosthetic and I confirm her question. Next thing I know she's rubbing my thigh and other parts of me, telling me she wants to see my fake leg. Raising my pant leg to show her, she stops me, telling me she wants to see the amputated part too. Well, one thing led to another.

"Okay baby. It's time for you to go on my leg and get some work done." I said to my old prosthetic, smiling broadly at that memory.

Getting myself connected and upright, I walk through the house. The drifting smell of what Hassan had for breakfast increases my hunger, but I see no food. There is nothing near the hot plates nor anything in the fridge but a damned radio.

"Damn, gotta go up to Barclay on an empty stomach."

Slamming the fridge door, a new food smell emerges. It's not as strong as Hassan's cinnamon plantains but it's a food source coming from a burlap sack in the corner. Rushing to it to open, I find maize, ginger root, fennel and apples, all in smaller burlap sacks.

"I'll eat his apples and pay him back later." I said, devouring them, thinking whether I should hail a cab or call for one to go find Hassan's amulet today.

I'm already dressed and don't have to gather up anything, so I head out the door to search for the stupid amulet. The gods are on my side, right now anyway. Two cabs are coming down Wolfe Street. One from the left the other from the right. Waving my arms to get either one's attention, the one on the right stops. I limp down the steps into the street to get in.

"Where to mister?"

"Barclay and 25th."

"Got it."

The ride there should take ten to fifteen minutes. I'll reevaluate the last few days and what can be my next move. Next move, what a joke. I have no idea what game is being played or pieces are being used.

The cab is slowing down, I see we're on 25th Street coming to the corner of Barclay.

"Damn my man, what you do run all the lights when I wasn't looking. Never mind, right here is good." I said, a little nervous about what I'll find in 3719. Not really sure why though.

I give the cabbie a ten spot for the $8.00 fare.

"Keep the change speedy."

"Thanks."

I slam the door shut, limping as fast as I can to cross the street, avoiding oncoming traffic. Several men standing on the corner in front of a closed liquor store check me out as I slow bound upon the curb. Their looks are meaningless to me. Except for the one who recognizes me.

"Hop-a-motherfucking-long cavity!" he shouts.

"You mean Cassidy, ya dumb fuck." another slurs.

"Yeah, him too." the other giggles.

They're drunk, continuing their stupor from two days ago or last night. Ignoring them, I keep on my way until the one that recognized me throws his unkempt body in my path. He has a debilitating smell of liquor, cigarettes and vomit that'll force your eyelids over your nose.

"Dude. What's happenin'?" You that bounty hunting son of a bitch with one leg and shit. What you doing up here, oh shit, you on a case ain't you?" he said, putting his finger up to his mouth to hush himself.

I move around this guy and keep limping by.

"Why you doggin' me and my posse man."

"My man, yeah, you're right. I'm on a stake out and need you and your posse to be quiet." I said.

"Man what Smitty mean by you got one leg?" asked one of the drunks.

"Shut up. He's on a stakeout." said Smitty, the one who recognizes me.

"Check this out gents, here's something to help y'all out." I said, pulling a fifty spot out of my pocket.

Stumbling closer to me Smitty snatches the bill from me. His boys swoop upon him fast, reaching for the cash. I make my get away up the street, trying harder not to limp the rest of the way in this old ass prosthetic. Don't want to draw any more attention to myself.

A few blocks away from Smitty and his happy homies, I make it to 3719. Death's been here, it's eye watering searing smell lingers. The house looks abandoned, as do the two on either side and several others on this block.

"I was here? This bounty must've been a big one then."

Before going any further, I check out the neighborhood. Recheck the house in question and the houses next to it. A lovey-dovey couple, all gobbled up in each other, walk arm in arm on the opposite side of the street. They're not paying attention to me or the music beating and rattling the car hoopty-ing up the street. Everything looks and feels clear to me, may as well get this over with.

Approaching the boarded up front door, death's territorial markings are stronger. Surprisingly, the front door, even boarded up, isn't that sturdy. Very easy to gain entry.

Inside, the front part of the house has pockmarks of dirt, empty liquor bottles, broken crack pipes and strips of ripped newspapers. Sunlight, straining to shine through filth stained windows, avoid pockets of darkness like the plague.

My dumb ass, steps into that darkness, landing onto something soft and squishy. Below me is a woman's breast. Her upper torso lays there, split in half at the waist. A collapsed wall covers the other half of her but drywall and wood couldn't split her like that. Looking a little closer, I see her body is torn or ripped.

"Wow. What the hell did that?" I said, moving further into the house.

More bodies are present. These were crushed by that falling wall. My nose picks up a smell different from Death's. Gunpowder and an explosive.

"Somebody blew something up in here. Maybe the wall was blown down not knocked down. But why? What the hell were they shooting at and trying to blow up?"

Gingerly, I amble around mutilated bodies to find more in the next room. Scattered, dust covered bloody bodies of men, women, dogs and rats, hundreds of rats lay in this freakish tomb. I hear a faint buzzing intermittent sound. Another damned thing to check.

"What kinda crazy shit happened in this house?" I said, picking up a plank to make a path through this unconnected meat.

I need to focus on why I'm here, finding Hassan's stupid amulet, but that buzzing is drawing me to the middle of the house. A large debris pile of broken wood, drywall, filthy ripped wallpaper, dead rats and a sneaker block my path. This sneaker, with the sole facing up to the ceiling, is connected to a leg embedded within the debris. There's something familiar about both the sneaker and this leg.

Being stupid, again, I walk over, swinging my plank at the leg knocking it over. No body attachment follows. It's a fake leg, my fake leg, next to my gun, knife, shredded clothes and a cell phone. The buzzing is the cell phones 'welcome' text message from the carrier which I promptly stop.

A bit unsettled, I place my stuff along with the old cell into my pocket then clear away more shit on the ground looking for the amulet.

"That shit ain't here. Maybe it's back there." I said, going deeper into the house.

I really should've just left the house. More bodies, different from the others. Different in that they are reaching out, the ones with arms anyway, to one another. It's like they're begging to be pulled away from something. My first thought is, 'all these rats did this', but they are chewed on and ravaged too.

Searching for the amulet becomes an afterthought. My new objective is to find out what or who did this and hope it or they ain't still here. I find more unhealthy carnage around the corner, five dead dogs, chewed and half eaten like the humans.

"If I was here, how come I didn't see any of this shit and why didn't whatever did this get me too?" I said, wondering how many people were here when this happened.

I find myself standing over a mangled man with his face half gone. The half that's left has an eyepatch scarcely clinging over his eye. For some reason, this guy looks familiar to me. I think for a moment then walk back to the area where my leg and other stuff were found. There's a crumpled piece of paper with the letters 'WA' showing that I saw earlier. Unraveling the balled up wad, the paper turns out to be a wanted picture of an Edgar Quali, the 'WA' is the beginning of the word 'WANTED'. Walking back over to the eye-patch man with the small wanted poster, I see that it matches. This guy used to be Edgar Quali.

"So. I was here for this motherfucker."

My new cell phone buzzes. Distracting me from Edgar and surprising me 'cause no one has this number. I look at the phone and it is a call.

"Hello?'

"Army Fuck. What's up."

"Derek?"

"Yeah douche-bag. What you do, forget about me?"

"Umm...no. Umm... what's up? How'd you get this number? You're not calling from The Store?"

"No shit Sherlock. I'm calling from the airplane, coming in from Vancouver. Your dumb ass text me from this phone Saturday night. You and numb-nuts Shaun get Edgar?"

I don't answer.

"Hey Army fuck, you hear me?"

"Yeah. I hear you. I got Edgar, looking at him now."

"Sweet. I'll be in Baltimore tonight, round 6:45 p.m.. Bring Edgar. He is alive right?"

"Yup."

"You and numb nuts bring him by at 9 tonight and I'll give you your cut."

"I'll be there without Shaun, he's dead."

"What? What happened, one of Edgar's boys got him? Sorry to hear that though but it's part of the job. See you at 9."

Derek disconnects. Good, I didn't feel like getting into it with him, plus I hear chatter outside the house.

"This is unit 17. Units 17 and 36 are here in front of 3719 Barclay. We're going inside to verify or deny dead bodies within the premises."

"10-4 Unit 17."

"Shit. Cops." I said, backtracking to the middle of the house to pick up my fallen prosthetic.

Needing to find a way out, I walk back to the rear of the house. The back door is boarded up tight with plywood and metal sheeting. Three dead bodies and several large rats add to the doors blockage. It'll take me a while and make too much noise to get through the door. I see the kitchen window has several loose boards.

"Last rat standing." I snicker as one flies out from under a box crate I slide underneath the window.

Getting up to the window was easy, removing the loose boards was a little tough. To start, I place my left palm over the pressure point of one of the boards to muffle the sound of breaking wood so they won't hear me. This board is heavy. Very awkward for me to remove it and balance myself without falling over. I've got three more to remove before they get back here to me. By chance, the boards were much looser and dry rotted so they weren't nearly as heavy or cumbersome.

Fitting my big ass along with this prosthetic leg under my arm through the window may be a lot tougher. The ten to twelve foot drop down from the window also might be a real bitch. No time to really think about it.

"Hello! This is Baltimore Police! We're coming in! Anyone in here!"

I fit the prosthetic out the window first then propel my body down out the window arms first, holding the prosthetic above my head like I would a rifle. Execution of the head first tuck and roll got me upright quicker and quieter than anticipated, especially with this old ass leg on. Stumbling forward, I maintain my balance heading into the alley avoiding these big ass crates in the backyard of the house next door.

Moving as fast as I can manage down the alley, I realize I can't catch a cab like this. Fake leg under my arm, limping out of an alley in the hood. A semi remote house further down the alley may be my saving grace. Trees, shrubbery and junk in its backyard will provide good cover for me to switch legs.

Sitting on a turned over shopping cart I undo my pants to get to my old leg. Just releasing these straps from around my thigh has my stump breathe better. Feels free, I guess pretty much like the feeling a woman has when she takes off her bra. I'll ask April when I see her.

The prosthetic I've been carrying slides onto my stump perfectly. Socket is snug, cool and comfy. The neoprene sleeve gives me more snugness, freedom and leg movement. I stand up, to get a feel. Nice. Much better.

"Universe is on my side right now." I said, looking around at the trash in this yard, trying to figure out what I'm going to do with this old ass bulky prosthetic.

I find a muddy, faded green duffel bag under some boxes and trash cans.

"Awesome find. This works out well."

After placing my old leg inside the duffel bag, I decide to walk back down the alley, towards house 3719. My nosey ass wants to see what's going on with the cops.

Ten houses away from the house, I hear the cops talking pretty clearly.

"Man, crazy shit happened up in here. This looks like that club last Thursday. Forbes you call Detective Norris yet about this shit?" an officer shouts out.

"Yeah. Him and HQ know. Damn man, I'm still counting bodies!" Officer Forbes shouts.

Hearing what's said has me feeling kinda good. Not bubble gum good, but hot tamale good. Not sure why the talk about all that killing excites me right now. Weird, very weird, but I need to get back to Hassan's to show him what I found. Then tell him I couldn't find his sacred amulet even though that'll piss him off.

I'm near the end of the alley, walking out on 25th Street, far away from 3719 and the cops. I walk and wait, and wait some more. Twenty five minutes go by, nothing. No taxis, hacks, or even a damned bus. I finally flag one down while walking East towards Greenmount Avenue. Back to Hassan's I go.

25 IF YOU SUMMON IT…

"Bout time you came back." Hassan huffs, from his kitchen as I open the front door.

I huff back, then walk through the foyer not saying a word. The two of us meet in the blood red room with all the pillows. Hassan has a large black gourd in his powerful ancient hands.

"Drink!" Hassan said, pulling out the cork, shoving the gourd into my face.

"Wait a minute old man. I just got in. Don't be pushing shit up in my face." I said, pulling away, dropping the duffel bag onto the ground.

"You will drink this. It'll change you into the beast then back into your human form for good. Drink! Drink Now!!"

Hassan gets closer and isn't stopping, so I stop him by clasping my hands around his forearms. Liquid sloshes around the gourd, spilling out onto us both and the floor. Hassan keeps his eyes fixed on me and his advancement, slower, never stops.

"Drink!" he yelled.

"Wait a minute. Last time you game me something to drink I slept for two days."

"Different type of drink."

"Relax old man, relax."

Hassan stops inching my way and I release my grip.

"You say this will make me turn into this werewolf thing then back into myself and I'll never be what you say I am again?"

"Yes. Drink!"

"This won't kill me will it? You said I'd stop being a werewolf when I die."

"No death, drink!"

I eyeball the crazed old African man holding a gourd with God knows what's in it. His gaze into me, never wavers as I lift the gourd to my mouth with him still holding it and take a small sip. Tastes like cranberry juice. Still staring at Hassan, I take a big swig then wait for something to happen. Having no idea what to expect, I start looking at my arms. They're still human. Touching my face, it's human too, as is my leg.

"Knew this shit wouldn't work old man. Told you a million times, I'm no damned werewolf!" I shout, bristling hard pass Hassan to get into the pale room, knocking over the gourd.

"You killed Shaun. You killed all those innocent people at Club 898. Allah only knows how many more you killed Saturday night." Hassan said, limping right behind me into the pale room.

"I did not kill Shaun!" I scream, turning to face Hassan.

Hassan draws back, face tightens. Pain and heat stop my advance. My stump burns, forcing its existence very bluntly onto my prosthetic socket. Loud, throaty, ungodly sounds are heard. I'm struggling hard to reason with myself, but those sounds skew my judgment. It sounds like they're coming from me.

Hassan backs hard into a wall stinging his higher level of consciousness. The sounds he's hearing are unfathomable. Harsh deep breathing in concert with bones cracking, human flesh ripping and stretching. Reticent to turn around, Hassan must eventually face the creature singeing its screaming soul. He must, for he's the one that conjured it up.

Facing it, Hassan's initial glance is in admiration. The werewolf looks approachable. Swiftly, reality shakes Hassan. He's taken aback in horror as the werewolf's snout extends, turning docile into frightening within seconds. That jet black wet nose grows longer, ugly, uninviting. Yellow impaling hellish eyes surrounded by fissure of black skin creates its face. The horrid coarse fur expands then retreats, entailing its hard sucking breathing. The werewolf fully itself, inspects Hassan, smelling his bouquet of fear.

In the distance the horse is heard thrashing around in the stable, twitching the werewolf's ears to attention. Hassan half smiles, crosses his arms gathering spiritual courage.

"My potion will soon change you back into the human you're supposed to be."

The werewolf mocking Hassan crosses it's hairy powerful arms, waiting. A few seconds pass with nothing occurring. The werewolf snarls heavily, sensing the confidence in Hassan fading. Languidly, the werewolf uncrossing its arms moves closer to Hassan. Sweat, once just beads, now fountain off of Hassan's powerful fearless face. The werewolf's deep, distasteful exhales, from its abrasive breath forces Hassan's sweat to roll upward.

"In the darkness, there's fear and comfort. Comfort embraces me. Allah loves all!" Hassan gurgles loudly before the beast masticates his face.

In a chaotic death tango with Hassan, the werewolf dips deeper into its meal with disturbed chews. The heavens become sullen as the ancient one is erased.

The hearty feast of the monster is interrupted by the maddening braying and knocking about of his horse in the stable. Infuriated, the werewolf rushes to the kitchen door with pieces of Hassan falling from its bloody snout. Its full mass obliterates the door getting out to the stable. Once again, neighbors are upset at the noise in the dusk of the day. Outpourings of profanity, anger and hate rage into the sky. That quickly ceases when all see a shadow of something other than the horse in the stable. Something large and towering raising a frightful arm, coming down hard and fast expounding an eerie slicing sound followed by a dull thud. Windows closed, shades are pulled down and curtains were drawn. If they had stayed and listened closely, they would've heard the unnerving sound of meat being raked off its core. The neighborhood playing peek-a-boo with hell is not a winnable game.

26 IT WILL COME

Serene soft chirps. An Oriole perches on the skylight above the foyer in Hassan's house.

"Damn bird waking me up? Shit, am I outside again?" I said, opening both eyes without any problems, this time.

"Oh shit!"

I'm in the pale room naked and legless with dried blood on my hands, chest and face. I quickly check my body for wounds, cuts or bites. None are found. This is how my ass was found in the park last week but I'm not as frantic or crazed. I wonder why. Also wondering who's fucking blood this is and why am I naked?

The smell of dead meat and cranberries helicopter through my nose. Where the hell is Hassan? My good prosthetic is on the bloody floor next to an old dirty duffel bag a few feet away from me. I don't reach for it nor call out for him, instead I crawl to the doorway to assess what's going on. The birds chirping has stopped. I advance on my hands and knees to the blood red pillow room where I too stop.

In front of me is a distorted, garbled, split body. Splashes of blood, bone fragments, books and skin are peppered on the floor, pillows, wall and ceiling. A closer look tells me, this was Hassan.

"Awww. man. What the fuck did this! Damn, damn, damn. Maybe that thing that attacked me last week is still alive. It got Hassan and not me, how? Why?" I shout, trying to get myself together to get the hell out of here before I'm blamed for this shit.

I start backing out of the room when I see what looks like words written in blood on the wall. It's hard to see on the blood red painted wall but I make out the word 'you'. Not grasping what's going on or what really happened, I just know I shouldn't be here.

"I hope that writing doesn't mean me. I couldn't have done that to him.

I'm no werewolf, they don't exist."

Huffing over and over, I make my way back into the pale room. I rush putting my prosthetic on. Luckily the white dashiki is still here and I put that on once I've righted myself to stand. I have no shoe and no time to look for one, but I grab my phone that's there. My gun and knife I don't see when leaving the pale room. Steadily, I walk through the room where Hassan lays avoiding the litter left by death to get to the kitchen.

"What the fuck!"

Inside the kitchen, the door leading outside of the house is destroyed. It wasn't a home invasion, I could easily tell his door was crushed from the inside with great force. No time to contemplate how or why. I've got to go. Rushing out of the house avoiding wood and glass with my naked foot, I completely forgot about the stupid ass horse, until now.

"Shit. He'll wake everyone up. Gotta take that chance it's asleep or won't hear me." I said.

Taking a few steps alongside the stable I hear a deadening creepy chewing sound. Could be the horse is too busy eating to notice me. Easing my head slightly to the front of the stable door I see the horse. It's on the ground in a large hideous lump. It's head, gone. What's left is being eaten by rats. A slow smile plates my face witnessing this melee. Another smile, this one bigger, erupts. There are overalls, a flannel shirt and boots in the stable next to a large pail of water. I go in avoiding the feast to wash the dried blood off of me and get the clothes. While changing I begin wondering if I did that to Hassan's horse.

With the overalls and tight fitting boots are on, I ease out of the stable. Lumbering down the alley I stop, thinking to myself about where the hell am I going.

"What am I doing. That shit with Hassan, I swear I didn't do that. I couldn't. But…..what if I did, what if I did. Oh my God, Shaun." I said, bent over from the frustration.

One minute I'm excited and crass about the terror I see, then I'm horrified. All at once I start running until my prosthetic and Hassan boots remind me I'm no sprinter. Looking around Hassan's hood I see I'm about three blocks away his house at the main street. There are a few people out doing their thing, not paying attention to a big black guy running down an alley with nothing chasing him.

"Bus ain't come yet homes. Due at 9:45 a.m., you got 15 minutes. You good?"

Talking to me is this tall teenage boy. High Top fade, bleached yellow old school Baltimore Neighborhood Basketball League (BNBL) under a red flannel shirt, way too long jeans, a knit backpack and purple canvas high top sneakers turned down at the ankle. I hadn't noticed but I'm at a bus stop.

"Yeah kid. I'm good. Ain't you late for school?

"Yup, had a booty call to take care of. Yo, why was you running, stopping, then turn around talking to yourself then run again and shit."

"You saw all that?"

"Yeah man, you scared two ladies away from the bus stop, but not me. I've seen shit like that before. My uncle did that shit. He was in one of those wars and he came back doing that shit you just did so I'm used to it."

"No I'm good kid. Plus mind your business." I said, slightly limping to the bus stop bench.

"Fuck you then man. Got no time for your stupid shit anyway, asshole." the teen said, boarding the oncoming bus.

Laughing, I sit down to relax against the graffiti laden bench. Bad move, as soon as my eyes close those images are back. The wolf-thing that attacked Randy and me, the craziness at Club 898, my fight with Shaun then a new flash of two elderly people in a car with blood geysering all over the dashboard.

Lurching forward, my eyes open to me alone on the bus stop. My need for comfort wants me to call April, but I can't. If I'm what Hassan and Shaun said I am then I definitely don't want to hurt her or get her further involved. I call Detective Norris instead. The phone rings.

"Northwest District, Sergeant Marshall speaking. How may I help you."

I'm hesitant to say anything but the officer hears me breathing.

"Hello! May I help you!"

"Yeah....Ummm can I speak to Detective Norris. I've got some info on the Club 898 killings for him."

"Sorry Detective Norris is not here today. I can take down the information and make sure he gets it."

"Off, no he can't be, not today. This is extremely important, it's a life or death thing that his cousin Shaun told me to tell him if he himself couldn't. Look I know Shaun is dead but I've got to speak to Norris. Can't you patch me through to his cell phone?"

"Sir I can't do that. Please give me your name and the information you have. I'll make sure Detective Norris gets it."

"No. I told you this is a life or death situation. Can you tell me where Norris is, I can meet him there or something?"

"Can't do that either sir. Like I said, any information you give me I'll be sure to get it to Detective Norris."

My frustration builds when I notice a folded newspaper under a brick on the bus bench. The page is folded to the classified section where the obituaries are. I see a small write up about Shaun's funeral. It's today at Cherry Crest 1st Baptist Church at 11:30 a.m. on Joh Avenue.

"Sir! Hello sir!"

"Never mind."

It's 10:15 a.m.. If I leave now I can make it there in 45 minutes by foot, in boots with a prosthetic on. It'll give me time to think about what to do and how to act once I get there. It's not going to be easy. Now's a good time for a stiff shot. Maybe I'll run into Smitty and his boys on the way.

27 RECKONING

My lonely walk to the church is a bitch. The only thing I can think about is what's really happening to me and why. The death of Hassan has me a bit disturbed as does the killing field up on Barclay. This shit, coupled with the mounds of the other larger shit, has me not thinking about what to do about the police who are more than likely waiting for me.

I make it, standing across the street from the church, hidden. The church's large brick dusty brown facade has a lower level with three glass doors where the mourners are entering. They enter through the middle door, the outside two are locked. The upper middle of the facade has a large stained glass window depicting Noah directing animals into the Ark. Not sure why, but my confidence builds as I see in the first group of animals being directed into the Ark are two Wolves. I grin and begin crossing the street, but duck back into my hiding spot. April and Kari come from around the right side of the church with Detective Norris coming out of the church middle door. In the foyer I see Detective Laboo, talking into his walkie-talkie. He's telling his men to be careful if they encounter me. I also hear Detective Norris's greeting April and Kari.

"Hi ladies."

"Cocamoe around?" April asks.

"No. Don't worry. If he shows up, Laboo's men will just detain and question him, that's all."

"So you say," said April.

Norris escorts them inside where they are met by Detective Laboo. Looking to my left up Joh Avenue, I see two patrol cars. Four officers standing outside of those cars, talking, looking around for me no doubt. Checking out the area further, I see on the right of Joh Avenue are three more officers. One's in a car, the other two are walking around checking alleys and the small park near the church. I've got to get inside the church

151

then worry about what'll happen afterwards.

Looks like most mourners have gone inside. Officers are staying at their posts. I start my crossing. Fifteen feet of me walking, nothing, so far.

I was almost to the curb of the other side when I hear several cops shout out,

"There he is! There he is!"

They converge on me as I make a staggered dash to the middle glass door. They order me to stop, drawing their weapons but not shooting. Mourners in the foyer screaming, running for cover get in my way. I do manage to lock the glass middle door. One of the officers tries to break the door with his staff, achieving only to crack the thick tempered glass. Other officers join in but the glass is too thick. I stop watching like a dummy when an officer decides to shoot the glass. Brawling my way up the steps through the throng of sinners, I'm met by three officers coming down the steps. I jump to a stop in the middle of the steps, waiting to be shot. Behind them are Norris, Laboo, April and Kari.

"All I want to do is say goodbye to my brother Shaun. After that, I'm all yours!" I shout out.

Detective Laboo squeezes through his men to face me.

"My men are at all exits. I'll let you pay your respects. I guess we owe you that much"

At this time, the officers from outside the church, are behind me.

"Stand down men. He's not going anywhere." Laboo shouts.

April fights her way to me, giving me a long awaited hug and kiss. It's cut short by Laboo pulling her away from me. He orders a path to be cleared for me to enter the main sanctuary. My frozen dark stare leaves him unfazed him as I walk by his officers opening the main sanctuary door for me.

Inside are many mourners, some known to me, some not. Nevertheless, all eyes gnaw at me as I focus on Shaun's black and silver coffin. The reverend looks down from his pulpit, shepherding me in.

"Bless you brother. Come on in, come on in. God's with you, Amen, Amen."

Hushed tones from the mourners become intense, almost unbearably to my ears. Shaun's coffin is closed. Why? Pissed the fuck off, I rush the coffin. Pulling open the lid displaying the distorted warped patched face of my partner, my brother, Shaun.

"Shaun I'm so sorry. My GOD I'm sorry Shaun. I didn't mean it. I didn't know. I didn't know!!" I shout, clenching my fists in agony, falling to my knees.

My actions sends the mourners racing from the pews to the safety of the officers in the rear of the church. My insides become hellfire, my stump shudders hard against my prosthetic socket. I need to sever these clothes from my blistering hot body. Straight away, I'm fully cognizant of what's happening to me. Hassan and Shaun were right.

My body, my God given body, contorts, thrashes and writhes in devilish pain, loosening my prosthetic. Rapidly tearing the overalls and prosthetic off, my body flops around the church floor in hysteria. The skin at the bottom of my stump explodes sprouting a bloody crackling tibia, quickly elongating outward into muscles, veins and tortured skin, forming a pulsating blood dripping leg.

Insatiable fur devours my new leg as it grows longer, along with my other fur encased leg. My anger and rage center on that inorganic piece of my God given body, my prosthetic. I hurl it to the rear of the church through that Noah and The Ark stained glass window. Shards of rainbow knives fall onto mourners and police below.

In viewing their demise, I see April. She's frightened yet bravely standing nearby, watching my suffering evolving into triumph. I've not yet fully changed, perhaps her great love for me has halted it. She reaches out to me in a gesture to help, comfort or console help me. Without warning, my head jerks fast downward. Uncontrollably, more of my bones creak, pop and snap as my growth ensues. April takes several steps away from me. Even more, when the face and upper body of Cocamoe is no longer.

Her prayerful scream begets an unrepentant howl from the werewolf. She turns to run to Norris, Laboo and Kari, but the werewolf pulls her back for a face to evil confrontation. It tilts down biting her from her chin to the top of her breast, coating the pulpit and front pews with her blood. The reverend, bewitched, faints, falling out of the pulpit. Pandemonium, anti-piety and repulsion baptize the main sanctuary. Officers, along with Detective Laboo, shoot into both the werewolf and April. Barbarically, the werewolf catapults Shaun's coffin at the offending officers. Some stop firing and duck. The airborne misshapen body of Shaun stops the others.

Behind the pulpit, molded to the wall, is a large statue of a cross with Jesus nailed to it. The cross has several large candles at its base with two long silver swords pointing skyward. The werewolf, with residual parts of April in its right paw, makes its way up the cross looking for a high vantage point or escape route. The remaining officers and Laboo keep shooting amid the mourners crying out God and Jesus's name. Detective Norris is loading his gun with bullets from the box in Shaun's truck.

"I hope this shit works!" Norris said, quietly, loading bullets laced with mercury, inside and coated with salt.

Norris fires two shots into the werewolf's back. Its deafening howl of pain echos off the church's high ceiling. It's climb up the prominent Jesus statue cross maintains, holding steadfast to the ravaged bloody shell of April. Norris fires five more mercury laced shoots, all five hitting its target. The earlier howls of pain recoup with what sounds like human screams of pain. It's paw releases April. Vestiges of her slam down into those decorative large candles at the statue's base. Her blood, intermingling with wax, fire and sections of her essence, spew into the choir area and pulpit. Kari, shrieking at the atrocity, faints into the rear pew. Norris takes aim at the werewolf as it's almost to the top of the cross, near a large air vent.

"Die motherfucker! Die!" Norris screams, emptying the rest of the mercury, salt laced bullets into the werewolf.

The monster stops climbing, grappling hard to hold on to the crucifix. Sixteen of Norris's special bullets have the werewolf's body smoldering with hell smoke from their entry points. An attempt to reach the top of the crucifix fails. The werewolf unceremoniously falls into the waiting blaze cocooning April. Fighting the fire, frenzied and turbulently. Imposing, April's scorched pimpled corpse to roll onto the spot where Shaun's coffin once rested. The werewolf's dying, debasing into the human it once was.

With great prudence, Detectives Norris and Laboo approach the newly created cremation chamber. Two officers hurry to extinguish the flames. All stare, in disbelief at the charred remains of both bodies.

"Norris, what in the Hell was that?" Laboo asked, solemnly.

"Werewolf." Norris said, covering Shaun's body with his coat.

"A what?" Laboo said, waving smoke and the stench of scorched humans away from his face.

"Werewolf. You know, man gets bitten by wolf, man turns into werewolf, goes on spree to kill, eat, kill, eat then kill some more. Typical Baltimore times are changing type shit." Norris said, holding tightly to a revived Kari, as they walk to the back door to leave the main sanctuary.

"Werewolves don't exist Norris!" Laboo screams.

"Ok, you tell that to all these witnesses and the press." Norris said.

"Norris! Norris!"

"Laboo! Your jurisdiction. Your clean up. I'm going home. Oh yeah, you might wanna chop that things head off to make sure it is dead!" Norris yells, closing the door.

Several officers and a few mourners still stand, shocked, at the amazement of what was just witnessed. Other mourners had bravely pulled the now awakened reverend from the area of the fiery pulpit. Minutes later there's a loud chopping sound followed by several shrieks.

28 EPILOGUE

Late Saturday night. Maycio and Hank, two Baltimore City employees working for the Department of Health and Animal Welfare, are on the overnight shift, drinking coffee. Their department collects dead stray animals from around the city. Autopsies are done by Baltimore City Health Department Veterinarians on these animals. They determine how they died and if their death is any threat to city residents in regards to viruses or diseases.

Maycio and Hank are watching TV intently when what sounds like a whimper is heard from the back room, where the dead animals are kept.

"Dude, what was that?" Maycio asked.

"How the hell should I know. Everything back there is dead." Hank said, laying down his coffee.

"Didn't sound like anything dead to me." Maycio said.

"Well, since you heard it, you go check it out." Hank said.

"What? You heard it too, man! Why me?"

"Seniority. Plus I ain't hear shit."

Maycio gives Hank a 'fuck you' look then stares at the door leading into that room. Inside this room are four dead animals, awaiting autopsies in the morning, a hawk, a fox, a rottweiler and a terrier. Maycio walks slowly to the door, not going any further.

"Hey, you might need this." Hank said, throwing a long plastic letter opener to Maycio.

Maycio catches it, snarls at Hank, then turns to open the door. He slides his hand inside quick, turning on the light. Slowly, he peers into the room viewing the four dead animals on four separate steel tables. Maycio stays at the door, going no further into the room.

"They're all here and they look dead to me!" he yells.

155

"You better go in and poke them to be sure." Hank said, sipping his coffee.

"Yeah, ok." Maycio said, frowning, proceeding into the room.

Wanting to do this quick and in a hurry, he runs into the room. Running pass the steel tables he pokes each animal with the letter opener fast, making sure not to turn his back to the dead animals. They never moved or made a sound as Maycio runs backwards to the door.

"You alright in there dude?" Hank yells.

"Yeah. I'm good."

Maycio relaxes. Smiling he turns his back to the steel tables to exit when his left arm is detached, rapaciously, feral from his body. His wavering, bloody squirting body turns to face his aggressor. It's the Rottweiler. The one shot and killed by Detective Laboo. The one that attacked and lost to the werewolf. The one, that's the new terror, to shepherd us all into hell.

THE END

(The Beginning)

THE SHEPHERD INTO HELL

ABOUT THE AUTHOR

Joseph's parents, Joseph Norris, Jr. and Gwendolyn Middleton Norris, took Joseph and his sister Dwauna to the Carlin's drive-in regularly to see scary terrifying films. Deemed by most too intense and frightful for any 10-year-old, Joseph loved them and was mesmerized by the horror. At the age of 12, the family moved from Cherry Hill to an area in West Baltimore called Beechfield. They still attended the drive-in and watched horror movies on the home VCR.

Joseph attended high school at prestigious Baltimore City College. At City, Joseph joined the storied family that is BCC, dating back to 1839, making connections that remain strong today. After High School, Joseph attended, Cheyney State College, a Historically Black College and University (HBCU), as it was called in 1982, now Cheyney University of Pennsylvania. Unable to meet the rising costs of tuition, Joseph transferred to Frostburg State University in 1984. Joseph regaled his suite-mates and others, with terrifying tales about the monsters in the woods surrounding the school.

In 1990, Joseph was involved in a near-fatal car accident, leaving him in a coma for three months. With the help of God, the Middleton/Norris, City College, and Cheyney Univ. families, his fiancée he eventually recovered. While lying in a hospital bed for six months, Joseph would tell his family the bizarre stories he imagined. Upon his release from the hospital, he married his college sweetheart.

After a year and a half of outpatient rehab, he returned to school, and received another degree in Computer Programming, thus beginning a new career in IT. Prior to finding employment, Joseph took a Creative Writing course at Morgan State University. He caught the attention of his professor, Dr. Eugenia Collier, with his first assignment. Naturally, it was a story replete with the macabre and complete terror he so enjoyed. Joseph had found his niche. He went on to write numerous short stories of which he shared with friends, family, and colleagues, all of whom encouraged him to publish his works.

Joseph and his wife gave birth to a son. He still dabbled with writing, but he thought of it as a more a hobby until he started writing a story he had thought of while in the hospital. That story, after six years, developed into the book, "The Shepherd Into Hell". Just as he was preparing the book for publication, darkness reared its ugly head in the form of kidney disease. After two year and seven months of dialysis, he received a call from Johns Hopkins Hospital that a kidney was available. With his wife and son in tow, Joseph rushed to the hospital to begin yet another life-altering experience. Not long after, the book was handed over to his publisher. Book number two is in the works, so be prepared. As Joseph says, "always be afraid of that creak you hear in the night."